# Black Beach

**Canada Council for the Arts**   **Conseil des Arts du Canada**       **Canadä**

We gratefully acknowledge the support of the Canada Council for the Arts and the Ontario Arts Council for our publishing program. We also acknowledge the financial support of the Government of Canada.

Cover design: Val Fullard

*Black Beach* is a work of fiction. All the characters portrayed in this book are fictitious and any resemblance to persons living or dead, is purely coincidental.

Library and Archives Canada Cataloguing in Publication

Guevara, Glynis, 1959-, author
    Black beach / a novel by Glynis Guevara.

(Inanna young feminist series)
Issued in print and electronic formats.
ISBN 978-1-77133-569-0 (softcover).-- ISBN 978-1-77133-570-6 (epub).--
ISBN 978-1-77133-571-3 (Kindle).-- ISBN 978-1-77133-572-0 (pdf)

        I. Title.  II. Series: Inanna young feminist series

PS8613.U483B53 2018              jC813'.6              C2018-904374-1
                                                       C2018-904375-X

Printed and bound in Canada

 **MIX**
Paper from
responsible sources
**FSC**
www.fsc.org  **FSC® C004071**

Inanna Publications and Education Inc.
210 Founders College, York University
4700 Keele Street, Toronto, Ontario, Canada M3J 1P3
Telephone: (416) 736-5356 Fax: (416) 736-5765
Email: inanna.publications@inanna.ca  Website: www.inanna.ca

# Black Beach

a novel by
## Glynis Guevara

INANNA
*Young Feminist Series*

*For my sister,*
*Caroline Guevara*

# 1.

BLAZING SUNLIGHT SCORCHED Tamera's limbs almost as much as the Trinidad moruga scorpion hot pepper she'd ingested after a dare from her older sister, Mary, charred her insides. She climbed into her father's car, and waved goodbye to her cousin, Azura. Tamera exhaled loudly, fanning herself with her hand. "It's really hot out here," she moaned.

"Like fire." Earl, Tamera's father, mopped up the sweat oozing down his forehead with a handkerchief he pulled from his shirt pocket. He swerved onto the street, veering left to escape a pothole. They listened to R&B, hip-hop, and soca music on the radio as he and his daughter headed home.

Earl pulled up at a red light and patted his daughter's knee. "Your mother's not doing too well this week," he said.

Tamera grimaced but didn't comment. Her mother, Alison, had been so sick so often lately that she was beginning to think her mom would never be back to her old self again. Although Tamera had thoroughly enjoyed spending the previous week at her Uncle Richard's home, she was more than ready to return to La Cresta, the rural community on the tiny Caribbean island where she was born. She hadn't seen her boyfriend, Dalton, in two weeks, and she was looking forward to spending time with him at the surprise birthday party his family had planned for his mother. The small gathering was scheduled for the following afternoon. She hoped her mother would be well enough to come as well.

She toyed with the ring Dalton had given her before relocating to San Pedro to work at a company that made fibreglass boats. To most people, the ring would have been considered a worthless piece of junk, but it meant as much to her as if the fake stone set in the middle was a ten-carat diamond. Every two weeks, Dalton made the tedious journey by bus from San Pedro to his parents' home, a ten-minute walk from her parents' humble abode.

Tamera lived a stone's throw from a two-mile stretch of sugary sand that extended offshore into deep, clear water and overlooked a purplish-blue bay littered with brightly-coloured fishing boats. The beach was one of the world's best-kept secrets. It had never been featured in any international travel magazine, and there weren't any swanky hotels, condos, or plush resorts in sight. Most villagers frowned at the thought of throngs of North American and European tourists invading their small community and frolicking half naked on the idyllic stretch of perfectly white sand. The villagers wanted their little-known hometown to remain a secluded location where shimmery fish darted about in the unsullied water and palm trees gracefully lined the shore.

Earl switched radio station halfway through a Kanye West song. A high-pitched beep sounded. "It's exactly one p.m.," a newscaster announced in a silvery voice. "We'll be right back with the today's headlines."

Tamera unwittingly tapped her left foot to the beat of a peppy soft-drink jingle as they waited to hear the news. The melody stopped, and the reporter announced, "An eighteen-year-old girl from San Pedro is missing." Tamera's lips stiffened as the girl's mother relayed how her daughter had left home to attend a job interview the previous morning and never returned. "Patty and I didn't have no problems. She didn't run away. She is a good girl, and I need the police to help me find her," the woman sobbed.

"What's going on here?" Earl tightened his grip on the steering wheel. "This is the second person from San Pedro that's gone missing in the past two weeks."

"I don't know, but it's scary," Tamara muttered.

Not long afterwards, Earl swerved into his driveway. Tamera got out of the car and walked purposefully toward her home, wincing at the loud music blasting from their neighbour Samuel Thomas's house. A porch with bright green balustrades encircled Samuel's home, a cheerful contrast to its bright red roof. Earl stood next to the bumper of his car, observing his son-in-law, Mary's husband's Renwick, pack a dingy, plastic bucket with soggy cement. Renwick handed the hefty container to his brother, Clyde, who lugged it up to the top of a wooden ladder. Clyde scooped a trowel full of the thick plaster and slapped it onto the exterior of the brick house that Earl had given Renwick and Mary permission to build on a plot of land next to Earl and Tamera's home. The land on which Earl's house was built, and several acres of adjoining farmland, had been passed down from Earl's grandfather, to his father and then to Earl.

Tamera's eyes fell upon the yellowish flowers scattered on the rounded canopy of an erect mango tree and the kidney-shaped fruit that hung from its long, string-like stems. Some of the stems had more than a few dangling fruit, others just one. The wind picked up, and the tree's dark green leaves with their distinct, horizontal veins slapped against the brick fence that separated their house from Uncle Charlie's. Tamera glanced at her Uncle Charlie's house on the right to see if anyone was home before she scooted up the staircase of her parents' home and slipped inside.

"You're back." Mary was sitting next to Tamera's mom, her head bent over a bowl of lentil soup, steam rising out of it as Mary blew gently to cool it down.

"It's you?" Alison said in a droning tone, lethargically passing her fingers through her full head of wavy hair that was equally silver and black.

3

"How are you, Ma?" Tamera gently kissed her mother's left cheek. Alison shrugged but didn't speak. Mary tried to slip a spoonful of the warm soup between her mother's lips, but she shook her head and clamped her jaw like an angry pit bull.

"You've gotta eat something, Ma," Mary pleaded, "or you're going to end up with a bad gas pain in your chest just like before."

Earl walked in and dropped into the chair next to his wife. He tried to coax her to eat as well, but his efforts didn't help. Alison's mouth remained tightly clamped. Tamera gulped down a tumbler of water and then headed to the bathroom for a quick shower. She changed into fresh clothes, and returned to the living room in a pink-and-white sleeveless cotton dress. Moments later, someone knocked on the door.

Earl turned to his younger daughter and said, "See who that is."

Tamera scurried toward the entryway, shifted the white, floral-patterned curtain to one side, and unlocked the door.

"How are you doing?" Dalton entered the living room with a massive smile.

"Good," she replied, her smile as bright as his.

He was as tall as a professional basketball player, so even though Tamera was five foot nine, she still had to lift her head to meet her boyfriend's sparkling light-brown eyes. "Good afternoon," he said, his eyes directed to Earl. "Pops asked me to return your drill."

"How's life in San Pedro?" Earl asked as Dalton handed Tamera the borrowed tool.

"No major complaints." Dalton's face fell a little. "You all heard 'bout the missing girl from San Pedro?"

"Yeah," Earl said. "I heard 'bout it on the radio on the way back from my brother's house earlier this afternoon."

"You know that girl lives a couple of streets from where I'm staying now. It's mind-boggling how she just disappeared." Earl and Dalton chatted amiably for a few moments before

Dalton suddenly spun around, gesturing for everyone to head outside. "I got a surprise," he announced, a wide grin on his face. Alison remained in her recliner, but everyone else stepped onto the porch. "There." Dalton pointed to a grey Mazda. "My boss's son got a new one, so I bought the old one off him. Now I can reach down here in next to no time."

"Hope you had a mechanic check it out," Earl said.

"Sure did," Dalton replied. "My brother's friend had a good look at the engine, and we took it for a test ride before I signed on the dotted line."

"Wonderful. You got a good car." Earl said, before going back inside.

"I've gotta run," Dalton said, his eyes on Tamera, "but I hope to see you all at Mom's surprise party tomorrow afternoon."

"Don't worry," Tamera answered for everyone. "We're all going to be there."

After Mary followed Earl inside, Dalton gingerly touched Tamera's arm. "You're going to email me some new photos?" he whispered.

"If you behave," she smiled.

"I'm always a good boy," he smiled back and winked. Then he jumped into his car and sped off, a whirl of dust rising up behind him.

# 2.

TAMERA'S MOTHER REMAINED IN BED most of the morning, and by two that afternoon the only thing she had managed to eat was a small slice of watermelon. "I'm going to stay home with your mother," Earl said to Tamera. "You go with Mary and enjoy the birthday celebrations." Tamera was about to protest, but loud voices echoing from the yard interrupted them.

Earl's nose and forehead wrinkled up like a crumpled T-shirt. "Mary and Renwick are fighting again," he sighed.

Tamera stuck her neck out the door just as her sister's husband hustled toward his car carrying a wailing Emma, his and Mary's daughter.

"Bring her back!" Mary shouted as she darted after him.

Renwick didn't answer. Instead, he moved even quicker and seamlessly slid Emma into the back of the car, then expertly buckled her in.

"Bring her back right now!" Mary screeched, her arms flailing as she tried to catch up with him. He sped off without looking back, Emma's wails smothered by the noisy exhaust.

Mary ran up the staircase and through the front door of her parents' house. "Renwick drives me nuts at times." She plopped into her mother's recliner. "His little sister has a nasty cough, and he still took Emma there, against my wishes." She closed her eyes, massaging her forehead as if she had the worst headache of her life.

"Why'd you marry such a jerk?" Tamera thought her sister could have done much better than marry a guy who didn't have enough ambition to find a better job than as one of their father's lowly-paid assistants. Earl even had to loan Mary and Renwick some money to aid in the construction of their home. Tamera was certain her dad would have to wait for many years before her sister and brother-in-law would be in a position to repay even a small portion of their debt.

"You'd better ask Dalton to come pick us up," Mary said, totally ignoring Tamera's comment.

"But it's only a ten-minute walk to his house," Tamera protested.

"I'm making a dish." Mary rolled her eyes. "You'd rather tote the bulky container over there than to ask him for a lift?"

When Dalton arrived the sisters were ready. They admired his new car, and giggled as they climbed in. Dalton revved the engine with pride. As they started to make their way to Dalton's house, they spotted two ten-year-old boys chasing a runaway kite in the middle of the street. Dalton had to swerve around them and he sounded his horn twice. When the car screeched to a sudden halt, Tamera's upper body tilted forward and seconds later the seat belt pinned her tightly to the back of her seat, almost knocking the air out of her chest.

"Woo!" Mary exclaimed, hugging the container of food on her lap.

"It's dangerous what they're doing," Dalton said, cautiously looking around before moving the car again,

"We used to do the same when we were their age," Mary snorted.

"True," Dalton conceded. "When I was ten, I took my brother's kite without permission and headed to my best friend's house. Unfortunately, the kite got stuck in a tree and I couldn't get it down. When I had to go back home, I was so nervous that I crossed the street without looking and almost got hit by a car. My brother told Pops that I'd taken his kite without asking, and Mr. Joshua also told him that I carelessly crossed the street. That afternoon Pops gave me the worst *cut tail* of my life."

"You're lucky we didn't have Facebook then," Mary chuckled.

"Facebook?" Dalton seemed confused.

"Didn't you see the video of the young girl getting a good licking from her mother for posting indecent photos on her Facebook page?" Mary said. "It was all over Facebook earlier this week."

"Oh, that!" Dalton pulled up in front of his parents' home, directly opposite a white house with verdant shrubs and an assortment of pink, red and orange flowers. The thick vines of an evergreen plant scaled the exterior of the modest home, creating a living wall. Copious bird of paradise with glossy green leaves and white flowers shaped liked pointed stars bordered the tidily kept yard. LaToya, one of Tamera's classmates, lived there.

Dalton's parents' yard, in complete contrast to the striking garden facing it, was entirely covered with concrete, except for a tiny circular area where a cashew tree with a short, irregularly shaped trunk blossomed. The branches on the tree waved vigorously as Dalton and his passengers got out of the car.

"Knock the door, 'cause I don't have no keys on me." Dalton patted his front and back pockets, looking up at Mary. She was on the top of the staircase, waiting.

"Tammy," Mary said, carefully holding onto the bulky dish. "Come and knock the door, please. My hands are full."

Ingrid, Dalton's sister, unlocked the door seconds after Tamera knocked. "Thanks so much for coming," Ingrid said, relieving Mary of the large pot, and gesturing to them to come into the house.

Just then, Jason, Dalton's brother, pulled up in a white Hyundai. He parked the car alongside Dalton's vehicle. "Hey," he waved, and then lifted a twenty-five-pound bag of crushed ice from his trunk, disappearing down the side of the house with the dripping bag.

Dalton's sister led Mary and Tamera to the living room, where George, Dalton's father, was sitting in a large armchair. "Where's the rest of the gang?" he asked, looking concerned.

"Pa stayed home with Ma 'cause she's still under the weather," Mary explained.

"I see," he frowned. Earl and George's friendship went back to their childhood. As young boys, they attended the same elementary and secondary schools, and if Earl hadn't dropped out in form four, in all likelihood they would have graduated secondary school together. Earl followed his father and became a fisherman, and likewise, George followed his dad and secured a job as a mailman. A short while later, Dalton's sister let in two middle-aged women. George looked across at Mary and Tamera, who'd by then settled on a big red sofa. "Meet my cousins from San Pedro," he said, introducing the newly arrived guests. "Excuse me, folks," he added a couple of minutes later. "I'm stepping out to pick up my wife. She's just finished work."

After the get-together, Dalton got into the driver's seat of his vehicle, and Tamera settled next to him. Mary slipped into the back seat just as he released the handbrake. "I hope you all had a good time," he said.

"I had a real nice evening," Mary said.

"Me too." Tamera sat back, closing her eyes, reflecting on the past hours she'd spent with him. Earlier that day, she'd made up her mind not to dwell on their impending goodbye. He reversed, and Mary gazed around the neighbourhood.

"Look at her outfit!" Mary snickered, her eyes on Cynthia, LaToya's mom, who was walking up a narrow concrete pathway in icepick heels and a tight-fitting, skimpy red dress. A full head of extensions tumbled down her back. Tamera stared at her classmate's mother, grinning.

"Have you all ever noticed the big tattoo on her arm?" Dalton asked as Cynthia shut her front door, disappearing inside.

"LaToya has one too, but it's on her chest. She showed it to us in the changeroom at school after gym class a few weeks back," Tamera said.

"Cynthia and LaToya are like two peas in a pod." Dalton rounded the corner, pulling up in front of Tamera's home a few minutes later. Mary's eyes widened the instant she spotted her husband's car parked in its usual spot.

"He's back," she said, rushing out of the car. She almost slipped as she shut the door.

Dalton's grin seemed effortless as he reached for Tamera's hand. "I'm going to see you in two weeks. In the meantime, send more photos, please. They make me feel so much closer to you when I'm in San Pedro."

Her face tensed. She could barely smile at him even as his warm fingers entwined hers. She wanted to bawl her eyes out but remained silent because she didn't want to draw attention to herself. "You've gotta send me more pictures too," she said softly, climbing out of the car. "I'm going to really miss you."

"Of course, I'm going to send you a bunch like I always do." He waited until she got to the top of the staircase before driving off.

Tamera watched the car vanish and later collapsed on her bed, lying face down on her pillow, muffling her sobs and wishing she could have gone to San Pedro with him. She didn't want to think about school, but there was no way to escape the new term, which was less than twenty-four hours away, or the CSEC exams that she would have to write at the end of the school year. The Caribbean Secondary Education Certificate was a big deal and she needed to pass with good marks if she hoped to move on to a higher degree. But Tamera really didn't know what she wanted to do after she finished school. The only thing that mattered to her these days was Dalton.

# 3.

TAMERA'S SCHOOL WAS BARELY a twenty-minute walk from home. She and her best friend, Jan, were form-five students. Jan was also Uncle Charlie's only daughter, and Tamera's first cousin. After school, they frequently made their way along Jonko Trail, which led to a perfect hangout spot close to the sea. This day in late February was no different. As they headed along the dirt trail, the salty air filled their nostrils and a refreshing breeze ruffled the thick canopy of green branches, tossing bits of dry sand around. Myriad butterflies fluttered around them and birds filled the air with song.

Liming at the beach was one of their favourite things to do. It was where they went especially when they wanted to talk privately about whatever was going on in their lives, things that were important or troubling. Jan's parents had recently separated, and she was having a difficult time coming to terms with the sudden change in her life. "I wish Mom would come back home," she moaned. "Life's not the same with her gone."

"I know you're having a rough time," Tamera said as her cousin's eyes watered.

"Mom could have at least asked me to go with her." Jan dried her moistened eyes with the back of her hand.

"Maybe your mom just needs time to deal with the situation, and then she's going to come back home."

"I don't think she's going to ever return," Jan said. "My family's destroyed for good."

11

As the girls strolled toward the beach, Tamera thought she better phone her sister, Mary. The call went to voicemail, and Tamera left a message. "You've got to stay with Ma a little longer today because I'm going to the beach with Jan," she said, leaving a message. Mary returned the call a few minutes later, but Tamera didn't answerpick up.

"She's going to be mad," Jan said. "You'd better call her back right now."

"Nope," Tamera said and smiled. "I'll call her in about an hour 'cause today I need a break."

Even though Jan's parents' marriage had fallen apart, Tamera secretly envied certain aspects of her cousin's life. For one thing, Jan's mother's mental faculties were intact, and she and her daughter could actually talk to each other about anything. Tamera couldn't do that with her mother.

Over the past year, Tamera's mother's mental health had deteriorated; her psychotic episodes lasted much longer and occurred with increased frequency. By late February, Alison had become deeply depressed and her sluggishness was taking its toll on the entire family. She'd lost a lot of weight, rarely got out of bed, and often complained of chronic pain. To prevent herself from breaking down over the state of her mother's health, Tamera dealt with her fears by escaping her presence. Hanging out on the beach always made her feel better.

When they arrived at the beach, the girls were shocked to discover a whale lying very close to the shore. A big wave must have rolled in, stranding the whale on a humongous rock. The large animal had pitched itself against the rock, trying to free itself from what looked like a net, entangled around its large body. "Let's call Mr. Joshua," Tamera said, scrambling to find her phone in her backpack. He was one of the most respected elders in the village and he would know what to do in this situation.

They watched helplessly as they waited, but by the time help finally arrived, the whale had died. They were the only girls on the beach as a group of men struggled to pull the sixteen-foot beast ashore.

"It probably got hurt by being tangled in that net," said Mr. Joshua. He and the men who had come with him examined the whale's body carefully for bruises. Earlier that week, Jan had read an online story about a whale in Thailand that had died after consuming more than eighty plastic bags and she wondered if the dead whale on the beach might have suffered a similar fate.

"The City Corporation's going to have to dig a hole to bury it," Joshua added. With all the excitement, the girls had lost track of time, but since Jan's dad had travelled to the city to attend a meeting and wasn't expected home until after nine that evening, she wasn't in a panic. Tamera had earlier responded to Mary's earlier call with a text message. "I'll be home by five," she had said, but it was already five -thirty.

Jan and Tamera lingered among the group of men on the beach who were discussing what to do with the dead whale. They were curious about the causes of the whale's death and what would be done with the carcass.

When Tamera's cell phone rang, she knew it was probably Mary.

"Where are you? You'd better come home right now." There was a familiar urgency in her sister's voice.

"Is it Ma?" she asked.

"Who else it could be, Tammy?" Mary said.

Tamera put her phone in her pocket, turned to Jan and with a heavy heart said, "Mary needs me, so I've gotta go."

"We're going to catch up later." Jan's eyes shifted from Tamera's face to the group of men, who were deliberating about how best to secure the dead animal from poachers.

It wasn't the first time Mary had called her younger sister in a panic. In fact, there were many such instances. One time stood out more than most; it had happened the previous month. When Tamera arrived home from school that day, her mother had locked herself in the bathroom and refused to come out.

As she stepped away from the water, and headed toward the unkempt trail back to town, she wondered what condition her mother would be in when she got home. She thought of her mother's mother and her father's sister, both of whom had suffered from debilitating mental health issues before their deaths. *Will I end up like them?*

Alison's mental health problems hadn't manifested until she was almost twenty-four and already married to Earl. *Is it a coincidence that three close members of my family have been stricken with this horrible illness?*

Tamera was fearful that she'd end up like her mother, and the more she tried to escape those thoughts, the more they persisted, causing her pulse to quicken and her head to pound.

Her thoughts flashed back to earlier years when her mother, though afflicted with bouts of mental illness, was able to enjoy her life and her family. Back then, on most carnival Sunday nights, the family would visit her Uncle Richard's San Juan home. On carnival Mondays and Tuesdays, they'd all participate in the festivities. During carnival time, her mother's spirit came alive. Tamera missed that spirit, that mother who seemed to love life so much then.

Things were different now. Every morning after Earl returned from his fishing trips, he usually rested, and the responsibility of taking care of Alison would fall on Mary's shoulders. During weekdays, Mary did most of the cooking, washing, and cleaning. She usually remained at her parents' house until Tamera got home from school. Tamera would make sure that her mom ate supper in the evening and she helped with the housework at weekends.

When he wasn't out on his boat fishing, Earl tended to his garden. He grew yam and dasheen and also Moruga hot peppers. He sold most of the spicy fruits to Joshua's wife; she made the hottest pepper sauce the villagers had ever tasted. Earl also had more than a few avocado, mango, sapodilla, plantain, and banana trees. Renwick and Clyde's duties, beside accompanying Earl to the open seas and preparing the nets, included wetting the seedlings and ensuring the bush on the family's property wasn't overgrown.

As time passed, Earl had become increasingly discontented with his earnings from the produce he grew when he measured it against the amount of hours he toiled the land. He hadn't discussed with anyone his desire to purchase a better fishing boat for himself, and then rent the older one to family members, but it was something he was considering. More importantly, he wanted to hire a caregiver for his wife in order to take some of the burden from his daughters' shoulders and he didn't have ready cash to do it. Several months ago, he had decided to put a plot of his land up for sale, but no one appeared willing to pay the price he was asking.

"You need to put it in a real estate agent's hand," Earl's younger brother, Charlie, had advised, but Earl insisted on finding a buyer himself.

Tamera stumbled over the uneven ground, trying to dismiss what she'd read on the internet days earlier about bipolar disease being a genetic disorder. "That will never happen to me." She repeated those words to herself over and over again, trying to convince herself.

Tamera suddenly wanted to turn back and almost did, but when she thought about how hard it was for Mary to take care of their mother day after day, she was s overcome by guilt. *Mary needs my help,* she reminded herself and she picked up the pace. She made the sharp turn onto Chester Street and, with only about five minutes' walk left to get to her house, she passed the familiar wide-open space in the neighbourhood where a half-dozen youngsters from the village were playing basketball. Her classmate, Joey, won possession of the ball. He floated in the air, and as thick dust settled beneath his feet, the ball sailed through a bottomless plastic bucket attached to a towering branch. Anton, another of her classmates, snatched the ball and dunked it. The makeshift net tumbled to the ground, and the agile youths, with joy on their faces, let out a series of deafening squeals and grunts. Joey's eyes met hers. He waved, and Tamera offered a feeble wave in return. As she watched her classmate play, thoughts of her sister and how close they used to be when they were younger flashed through her mind. The two of the them used to play in that open field all the time.

An incident involving the decomposing carcass of a dead horse that had washed ashore several years earlier came back to her. The authorities believed the animal had been dead for over two weeks. A backhoe couldn't reach it to pull it out of the water, so it had to be cut into pieces in order to be removed and then properly buried. The principal at La Cresta Secondary dismissed school classes early one morning when the pungent odour of the decaying horse had wafted into the school building. That day, Tamera arrived home much earlier than usual and when she opened the door, she had been surprised to see Mary sitting at the table with her parents deep in conversation. "Me and Renwick are getting married because I'm going to have his baby," Tamera heard Mary say. Up until then, Mary and her younger sister had always traded secrets before revealing them to anyone else. On that day, Tamera realized her relationship with her sister had changed.

As she got closer to home, she heard a familiar soca tune blasting from Samuel's residence, but the music was several decibels lower than usual. Samuel's brother, Edgar, who'd lived a semi-reclusive life for the past ten years since his wife died, was walking ahead of her, his left leg as stiff as if it were made out of wood. Tamera thought he smelled like sweat and rotten eggs mixed together, so she slowed down until he entered his yard, which was next door to his brother's.

It was a tradition in the village that several months before carnival, Samuel would set up a mini mas camp in his front yard, a place where villagers could come and help create handcrafted carnival costumes. People had already started working on them for the upcoming festival. Tamera walked past partially completed carnival costumes that were on display on a workbench in front of a tiny shed. Some of them were adorned with batting fabric and feathers, others with sequins and decorative braids. Their brilliant colours shimmered in the sunlight. Neither Samuel's daughter, Georgina, the perpetual carnival queen at La Cresta Secondary School's annual carnival celebration, nor her brother, Tamera's classmate, Delroy, were with their father and several others toiling over the kaleido-scopic costumes.

A sign posted at eye level on Samuel's front gate read, *Wire-Bending Classes Available.* Samuel was an expert at making the frames for grand Ccarnival costumes. For several years, he'd been offering classes in the village to teach young people how to make the curves and shapes for costumes with wiring. These sessions were available at a nominal fee to the youngsters in the village, but this wasn't a skill Tamera was interested in developing.

"The art's dying," Samuel said time and again. He thought it was important to pass his skills on to the next generation. He was one of the happiest people Tamera had ever met, and unlike his brother, he was always dressed flamboyantly in bright, patterned shirts and equally bright trousers. The annual carnival parade was scheduled for early March. There were only two weeks left before the vibrancy that filled Samuel's home and yard every night until way past midnight would finally subside.

"No, Ma, no! You can't go outside like that!" Mary's voice quivered as Tamera fumbled to open the front door. Tamera slipped inside, and immediately caught the attention of her mother's wretched eyes. Alison's facial expression said more to Tamera than she was willing to admit to herself. She tensed, stunned by what she saw and she was unable to put one foot in front of the other. Alison was rushing about the house completely naked while Mary sped after her, anxiously trying to drape a housecoat over her mother's body.

"Don't stand there!" Mary bawled. "Come and help!"

Neither Mary nor Tamera understood their mother's babbling. Tamera ran toward her and she and Mary struggled to restrain Alison as she lunged for the side door. Abruptly, she relented and collapsed on the floor, allowing them to slip on her undergarments, and then the housecoat on top. They kept a close eye on her until Alison's younger sister, Leila, arrived at the house.

Tamera stood next to her aunt's Volkswagen Touareg, cuddling Mary's young daughter, Emma, and observing her mother's arms and shoulders drooping like an ape's. Leila, in a pair of blue jeans and a tie-dyed T-shirt, moved with a manly gait, leading Alison to her white car. She had a trim and muscular body, as buff as a man's. Her nieces had never seen her dolled up with make-up, not even a touch of lipstick, nor did she ever wear a dress or a skirt. Mary placed a bag with her mother's toiletries and some clothing in the trunk.

Leila patted Tamera's shoulder, attempting to offer some comfort, the distress on Tamera's face was palpable. "Your mom needs help, and I'm going to ensure she gets it," she said. Tamera stood expressionless and silent, staring blankly at her aunt's bushy eyebrows with their tinge of grey.

*Why do I have a mother who is not well?* Tamera thought as her aunt drove off.

"Ma's going to eventually get better and come back home," Mary said as Tamera handed her Emma.

"Ma's never going to get well!" Tamera yelled as frustration gnawed her insides. "Aunt Leila's taking her back to the mental hospital, where they're going to drug her up, and then they're going to send her home, and then she's going to act like a zombie again, and after a while she's going to stop taking her medication, and we're going to be in this same situation all over again." She slipped past Mary and flew through the front door, bursting into tears.

"Tammy!" Mary shouted, but Tamera ignored her. "Tammy!" Mary repeated with urgency, rushing after her sister, clutching Emma in her arms. Tamera slipped inside her bedroom and slammed the door. "We need to chat. There's stuff I need to tell you." Mary stood mere inches from the closed door.

"Tomorrow," Tamera cried, trying to muffle her tears.

"Okay, tomorrow then," Mary said.

Tamera sat at her desk, staring out the window at the darkness that had crept over her. Mary's footsteps became distant, and there was a soft thud as she shut the front door. A mosquito buzzed close to her ear, making Tamara itchy. She swept the air with her hand, and booted up her computer. She downloaded several pictures Dalton had emailed her earlier that day and admired them, wondering if she would ever have the courage to send him the photographs of her that she knew he wanted. But she brushed that uncomfortable thought from her head, and for the next couple of hours she lost her thoughts playing her favourite online typing game.

Early the next morning, before she was fully awake, Tamera sensed her sister's presence at the foot of her bed. "You're not going to school today?" Mary nudged her playfully.

"What do you care?" Tamera muttered, and turned her head away, keeping her eyes shut.

"You'd better get up and get ready," Mary said as she shifted the heavy drapes to one side, allowing the light to stream through the big window.

"Pull them back!" Tamera groaned. "I need ten more minutes."

"You play computer games too late at night, and that's why you can't get up in the morning." Mary poked Tamera's arm again. "You're going to be very, very late."

"Who cares?"

"I do."

"And what if I refuse to get up?" Tamera vehemently jerked her head from right to left. "You can't tell me what to do. You can't order me to get out of bed if I don't want to."

Mary tried hard to placate her sister. "Hey, I made breakfast, scrambled eggs and toast. And you can come home for lunch, since I'm going to have hot food ready for you."

"Why should I come home for lunch?" Tamera said, sliding grudgingly out of her bed. "You know that I never, ever come home during lunch break."

"I thought you might want to eat something different, something better than a boring sandwich."

"My sandwich is never boring," Tamera said with a frown. She sat at the foot of the bed, and bowed her head in despair. "I hate coming home. I hate this house!"

"Okay, then," Mary said. "I'm going to have hot food ready by three-thirty."

"I am not coming straight home after school!" she yelled.

"Okay, Tammy," Mary said softly, "just calm down. I'm in pain too. I love Ma just like you."

"Me and Jan are going to hang out by the water, so don't expect to see me before sunset," Tamera replied firmly.

"Whatever." Mary stepped toward the door and then abruptly spun around. "You want to know a secret?" she asked. Her face lit up as if she had good news to share.

"But you never share any secrets with me anymore. Why now?"

"Come on, Tammy. That's not true."

"Yes, it is."

"This is good news. You want to know or not?"

"Know what?"

"You promise not to tell anyone for at least a couple of months?"

"I'm not a tattletale."

"Okay, here goes," Mary said, a wide smile on her face. "I'm going to have a baby."

"Another one?" Tamera said. "But Emma's still so young."

"It just happened." Mary shrugged. "We didn't plan it."

"You going to end up with a string band of kids by the time you turn thirty," Tamera snorted, then put her hand over her mouth to suppress her laughter.

"No way." Mary massaged her flat belly. "This is going to be the last one."

"I hope it's a boy," Tamera said.

"That's what Renwick wants, but I'm longing for another girl."

"Well, I hope you're happy."

"You hope?" Mary paused for a second. "I don't look happy?"

Tamera remained silent and Mary stepped toward the door. "I'm going to check on my daughter," she said, gently closing the door behind her.

It had been ages since Mary shared even the tiniest secret with her younger sister, and Tamera secretly blamed Renwick for the distance that had formed between them. She loved Mary and wished she'd fulfilled her dream of becoming a dietician. Mary used to speak with so much passion about training for a job that would allow her to advise people about how to eat properly, but with a young daughter, a second baby on the way, and very little money, Tamera feared her sister would get bogged down in life and eventually abandon her dreams.

*Will Mary's unborn baby inherit our family's bad genes?* That thought crossed Tamera's mind as she pulled out a chair in the kitchen, and prepared to eat breakfast, but she didn't share her feelings with her sister.

After swallowing a few mouthfuls of porridge, she called her cousin, Jan. "You'd better go ahead, 'cause I'm going to be really, really late." But when Tamera finally stepped out the door, Jan was standing at the gate with a big grin. Also, Earl's van was parked at the front of the house. Tamera was surprised that her dad was at home when he should have been out selling his catch to the villagers, but it was too late to go back and knock on his bedroom door to see what was up and why he was at home.

"What you doing here waiting for me at this late hour?" Tamera asked.

"I didn't want to leave you behind."

Tamera and Jan entered the school compound, immediately making their way to their English literature class. "Young ladies, you're late again!" Mrs. Miles, the teacher looked like a big cat ready to pounce on them. The girls quietly took their seats and opened their textbooks.

Tamera was due to write the CSEC exam, her high school equivalency examinations in May and June, and was doing fairly well in English language and literature, and biology, but her chemistry, Caribbean history, and economics marks weren't up to par. The mathematics score she'd received on the last test was much lower than that of any of her other subjects, and she wanted to drop it, but it was compulsory, and her math teacher wouldn't hear of it. Overall, students she'd consistently done better than in the past were now doing considerably better than her, and even though Tamera was keenly aware that she needed to spend more time studying, she lacked the motivation, and couldn't explain why it seemed that everything had suddenly become so difficult.

# 4.

AFTER SCHOOL, JAN ASKED, "What time do you want us to head to Mr. Samuel's place?"

"About five-thirty," Tamera replied as she unlatched the gate.

"See you then," Jan called out before heading for home. Tamera waved and then ran up the staircase two steps at a time.

"Pa, "what happened?" she asked as she burst into the living room. She rushed toward her mother's recliner, where Earl was sitting with a bandaged arm.

"Just a little accident on the rough water," he said and touched his bound arm.

"You went to the doctor?"

"The health centre." He paused for a moment, then took her hand. "How's school?"

"Okay," she shrugged. "As usual, it's nothing special." She made her way to the kitchen and dished out a large plate of food from the pot, and after chowing down the rice, beans, and chicken Mary had prepared, she dropped her books on top her bed and slipped into the bathroom to shower.

Later, she came back to the living room wearing a fresh pair of blue jeans and a cotton T-shirt. "You're going to Charlie's house?" Earl asked as she stepped toward the front door, and slipped into her sneakers.

"No, Pa." She turned, looking at him. "You forgot 'bout Mr. Samuel's wire-bending exhibition?"

"Oh," Earl nodded. "Is it today?"

"Yes, Pa. I'm going to hang out with Jan and my other friends there." She noticed her father's doleful eyes, and added, "Why you don't come with us?"

"I don't think so. You go and have fun." Earl waved her away with his good hand. "I'm going to stay right here in front of the television and rest this arm."

"Okay, Pa." She waved then hurried out of the house.

"Watch out!" Mary yelled as she and Tamera bumped into each other at the door of the house. Emma had almost slipped out from her mother's arms. "You rushing out of here like you going to see some big soca artist like Machel, Bungie, or Faye Ann Lyons," Mary laughed.

The bouncy music was at a moderate volume when Tamera and Jan walked through the wrought iron gate at Samuel's place. Earlier that day, a few of the villagers had helped Samuel erect a large white tent in his brother, Edgar's yard.

"Let's go in," Jan said, pointing to the tent.

There was no fence separating the two properties, so the cousins casually walked from Samuel's yard to Edgar's and into the tent where they immediately spotted their classmate, Cassandra. She looked up at Jan and smiled. "I was just this minute going to phone you," she said, pocketing her phone. "Look at the headpieces I made." Cassandra identified her three creations from among the costumes on display inside the tent.

Tamera heard her name called and spun around to see four more of her classmates striding into the tent and grinning. LaToya, in a sleeveless crop top and very short shorts walked slightly ahead of her three companions.

"When did you do that?" Jan asked and pointed to LaToya's exposed white opal belly ring.

"Last weekend," she said.

As Jan reached out to touch the piercing, LaToya shuffled

sideways. "Don't," she said, her hand guarding her belly. "It's still quite sore, and I don't want it to get infected."

Someone turned up the music, and for a while the girls could barely hear each other's voices. More of their class-mates arrived, and eventually eleven of them were liming together in the yard, admiring the colourful costumes and enjoying the music. "This village is always so dead except for carnival time," Jan said. "It's real good to see so many people supporting this event."

"Yeah," Tamera nodded. "There're tons of people here that I've never seen before."

Cassandra squinted, staring in the distance. "What you looking at?" Jan asked.

"Over there," Cassandra pointed. The girls watched a young couple unknown to them. The young man had placed his girl-friend's back against a tree, and they were kissing each other and laughing at the same time.

"They're having fun," Tamera giggled.

Jan poked Tamera's waist with her elbow and whispered, "Look over there," pointing to a corner in the left where the crowd had thinned.

Tamera's eyes shifted toward Samuel's brother, Edgar, who was standing slightly apart from everyone else. He had a half-empty bottle in his hand and he looked drunk. Tamera shook her head. "I don't like that man," she said to Jan. "He gives me the creeps." She watched him as he turned and stumbled toward his own house, stepping clumsily through and side door and disappearing inside. *Good riddance,* Tamera thought, a shiver running down her spine.

"Come closer people!" Samuel invited the patrons to gather close to the tent, where his more accomplished students demon-strated their newly acquired skills in the art of wire-bending.

By the time the wire-bending exhibit ended, at least fifteen more people had show up. The classmates then huddled together near a concrete bench, and talked about their schoolwork, their friends, and just about everything else that was going on in their village. LaToya stood slightly apart from the group, flirting with a young man, Richard, who had been in the same class as Tamera's boyfriend, Dalton.

A tall, slim man in his early twenties swaggered past the concrete bench in a red T-shirt and dark jeans. "Wow," Jan said, admiring him. "Who's that?"

The young man ran his fingers through his short, wavy hair, and his smile widened when Cassandra giggled and he noticed the girls next to her gawking at him. But he didn't stop to chat. He continued toward Samuel's son, Delroy, who was standing with some friends not too far from Tamera and her friends. The girls were close enough to hear them although they were trying hard to look as though they were not interested at all.

"What's up, cuz," Delroy said.

"Fine, thank you," the handsome young man said. "How are you doing?"

"Great," Delroy said. "But I've gotta introduce you to someone."

LaToya's eyes shadowed the young man as he and Delroy hurried across the yard. She stepped closer to her friends and said, "He's kinda cute. Any of you guys know him?"

"You're talking 'bout Delroy?" Cassandra snickered, keeping her voice low.

"Come on," LaToya said. "Delroy's our classmate. There's nothing special 'bout him. I'm talking 'bout that hunk in the red jersey and black jeans."

"Ask Tamera or Jan," Cassandra chortled. "They live on the opposite side of the street, so they know more than us."

"I don't have a clue," Tamera smiled.

Jan giggled. "Me neither."

"I'm going to get his number before this evening's up, just watch me," LaToya said as she turned and quickly followed Delroy and his cousin.

She returned about ten minutes later. "I didn't get a chance to talk to him," she moaned. "By the time I caught up to them, the hunk was talking to a girl by the gate. And Delroy wouldn't introduce me!"

As the evening progressed, Jan and Tamera's classmates split up into smaller groups, strolling around the grounds in groups of twos or threes. When Tamera and Jan headed to the washroom, they watched LaToya clowning around and flirting with a number of the young men at the party. "LaToya's just being LaToya," Jan said as they watched their friend playfully slap a guy's butt.

"You know who he is?" Tamera said.

"Not a clue," Jan said as the man spun around, smiling heartily as he wrapped LaToya in his arms. Her knees were slightly bent when he swept her off the ground.

"She obviously knows him," Jan said.

Tamera nodded. "I realize that."

After they came out of the bathroom, they teased LaToya about her conquests.

"You only live once," LaToya laughed then hopped off the bench they were sitting on. "I'm off," she said and disappeared into the crowd.

The girls danced under bright artificial lights, swaying and shaking their hips for much of the evening. At about eleven the crowd began to thin out.

"It's time we get going," Cassandra said to her friends. The classmates all lived within ten minutes of Samuel's house and had earlier agreed to leave together.

"Where's LaToya?" Jan asked as they gathered at Samuel's gate.

"I haven't seen her for at least twenty minutes," Tamera said.

"More like half an hour," Jan said.

"The rest of you wait here," Cassandra said. "Me and Jan are going to walk 'round the yard and look for her." The two girls searched the thinning crowd without success.

"We can't figure out where she's gone," Cassandra shrugged when they got back to the group.

"You all checked the washroom?" Tamera asked.

"Yeah. We did," Jan said. "No one was in there."

"She probably left already then," Tamera said.

"I guess," Cassandra said, but she looked concerned. She was a closer friend to LaToya than any of the others. "I'm going to call her cell right now," she added. She punched in LaToya's number, pressing the phone to her earlobe. "Come on," she said impatiently, waiting for LaToya to answer. "It's gone straight to voice mail." She scowled, and pocketed the phone. "I'm going to try again when I reach home."

The outdoor light at Tamera's home was shining and the front door was unlocked when she got back.

"You had a good time?" Earl was still on the recliner.

"Yes, Pa. It was a nice evening," she said and headed straight to her room.

About ten minutes later, she received a text from Dalton. *Pleasant dreams my love,* she texted back.

Then her phone rang.

"Cassandra just called to tell me that LaToya's still not answering her phone," Jan said. "She wants to call her mom, but she doesn't have her new cell number."

"She's crazy or what?" Tamera said.

"Why'd you say that?"

"Cassandra wants to tell LaToya's mother that LaToya didn't leave with us. Why Cassandra wants to snitch on her friend?"

"But what if something's wrong?" Jan said. "Her mother should know what's going on."

"LaToya's probably busy doing what LaToya does best," Tamera giggled. "I know that you, Cassandra, and LaToya are closer friends than LaToya and me will ever be, but you and Cassandra are worrying too much. Get a good night sleep, and we're going to talk in the morning."

"I guess you're right."

"Good night," Tamera said. "Sleep tight."

"Why aren't you answering your phone?" Jan's voice was strained when she hurried inside Tamera's parents' living room at exactly nine-thirty on Saturday morning. She had a concerned look on her face that also wore a big frown.

"I didn't hear it ring," Tamera explained.

"But I tried to reach you twice and ended up leaving two messages."

"Gosh," Tamera said, checking her phone. "I don't know how I didn't hear it." She looked at Jan quizzically. "How come you here so early? What's wrong?"

"LaToya never went home last night," Jan said.

"She didn't?"

"Nobody knows where she is."

"You're sure 'bout that?"

"Cassandra phoned me early this morning," Jan said. "She told me that LaToya's mom called her around twelve-thirty last night to find out where LaToya was, and up until ten minutes ago she hadn't reached home yet."

"You're joking, right?" Tamera laughed nervously.

"No, I'm dead serious," Jan said. "I'm real worried that something happened to her."

"Happened to who?" Mary walked in.

"LaToya didn't go home last night," Jan said.

"You all know that LaToya is a hotspot," Mary said. "She's probably having a good time wherever she is, and you all are here worrying."

"Why are you always thinking the worst 'bout everybody?" Jan snapped, the stress lines on her forehead deepening.

Mary sucked her teeth and stepped toward the kitchen. She wasn't going to respond to that.

"You never have nothing good to say 'bout nobody," Jan's voice cracked as she raised it.

"You all have short memories or what," Mary snapped, looking back at them. "You all already forgot that she left home for a whole week last year, and during that time her mother didn't know where she was."

"That was different," Jan said. "She and her mom had a big fight, and that's why she went to her cousin's house."

"Yeah, right," Mary said. "That whole tale 'bout her staying by a relative was a cover-up. I know what I'm talking 'bout." Mary took a couple of steps toward them then stopped. "I bet you all that she's going to show up in a couple days and act as if everything all hunky-dory."

The news of LaToya's disappearance spread quickly throughout La Cresta. "How could somebody go missing from a tiny place like this, and nobody hasn't seen nor heard nothing?" Earl grimaced when he heard the news.

LaToya's mom, Cynthia, was several years younger than him, but they were both life-long residents of La Cresta, and in that small community everybody knew everybody.

"I'm going over there later today to show my support," Earl announced the following morning.

"I'm coming too," Tamera said.

"If you want to walk then you're welcome," he said. "'Cause I'm not taking the car."

"Not a problem," she said.

That Sunday in the early afternoon, Tamera and her dad walked down Chester Street in the torrid heat. "You've gotta go through this story again," Earl said, questioning Tamera about what she'd observed at the wire-bending exhibition. The police hadn't questioned Tamera or any of her friends, but her father was acting like an investigator.

She exhaled. "There was a big crowd, and I didn't know half the people I saw LaToya talking to," Tamera said. "We didn't realize she was gone until close to eleven, when we were getting ready to go home. I hadn't seen her for at least half an hour before that."

The street in front of LaToya's home was congested with vehicles, and Tamera quickly figured out why her dad had decided to walk. "I really hope nothing bad happened to that girl," Earl scowled, unlatching Cynthia's gate.

"I hope so too," Tamera said and bit her lip. There were about a dozen adults and three children on Cynthia's tiny porch, some standing, others sitting, but the dozen or so folks ceased their chatter, inspecting Tamera and her dad as they wiped their feet on the stiff doormat.

"Good day, good day, everyone," Earl said in a powerful voice. The men and women who were on the porch almost answered in unison. Tamera's eyes swept over the crowd, but Earl directed his eyes straight ahead and entered the house. Tamera followed in silence. They felt the heat and the sadness in the living room the moment they got inside.

"Thanks for coming," Cynthia's voice was brittle. She swallowed hard, pressing her hand on her throat, her rheumy eyes on Earl's face.

"How are you holding up, girl?" Earl said as he embraced her.

"I don't know," her voice cracked. "I'm trying to be strong." She paused. "But it's killing me on the inside. I want my child to come home so that everything can go back to normal."

Cynthia ran her hand over her long hair extensions neatly held in place by an elastic band. She switched on the standing fan. The swirling breeze twirled the wide skirt of her blue cotton dress and ruffled a few errant strands of hair on the top of her head, as well as the thick, long mane flowing down her back. The curtains over the doorway came to life, flapping violently.

Cynthia was a poor reflection of her former self. The bubbly woman was gone. Her usually made-up face was bare and she wasn't wearing any of her usual brightly-coloured earrings and bangles. The only familiar bits of her old self were the stud piercing on her left nostril and the lion and flower tattoos boldly displayed on the upper portion of her slender arms. Her living room was as neat and tidy, as was the rest of the house and even the outdoor garden.

"Have a seat," Cynthia's sister, Molly said as she led Earl and Tamera to an off-white sofa in the middle of the room.

"Sis," Molly gestured, "Please sit down."

"I'm good," Cynthia remained standing, puffing on a cigarette.

Tamera sat before her father did, and slid over to the left-hand side of the sofa. Earl sat on her right, recalling the news he had heard on the radio several weeks before about the missing San Pedro girl who never made it home following a job interview. There were still no traces of that girl or of several other young women who had vanished on the island during the past months. He dared not mention any of this to Cynthia.

"I called her cell phone a million times already, but she's not answering," Cynthia said and held her chest, worry etched on her face.

Earl rose from the sofa. "Please sit," he said and gently took her right arm.

"Okay, okay." She slowly bent her knees. After settling on the sofa between Earl and Tamera, she entwined her fingers, struggling to keep her composure. She finished the cigarette and right away lit another.

"The first couple of times I called her cell it was going straight to voice-mail, but now a recording telling me it full up, and I can't leave no more messages." Cynthia lowered her head, and placed her right hand against her temple, her palm wide open. She lifted her head, and fixed her eyes on Earl. She promptly bowed her head again. "The police in this country are a bunch of jokers. When me and Molly went to the station to make a report, they didn't take what we told them serious at all. Even though they wrote down what we were saying, they didn't really offer no help. They told us point blank that LaToya probably ran away. Have you ever heard such stupidness in your life?"

"I'm real sorry 'bout that," Earl said. "I wish there was something I could do to help."

"We're having a vigil tonight on the empty plot of land close to your place."

"If I didn't have to work, I'd surely go."

"I understand," Cynthia said. "All I want is for my daughter to come home." She swallowed. "A lot of people are gossiping that my child ran away with a man, but that's a lie. Tomorrow is her birthday." Cynthia pulled her lips between her teeth. "Look over there." She pointed to a neatly wrapped parcel on the shimmering hardwood floor. "I have her present waiting for her."

Tamera remained almost completely still, recalling several instances when she was so overwhelmed by her mother's illness that she'd longed to disappear from La Cresta, but as she observed Cynthia's trauma first-hand, she was glad she'd never built up the courage to run. And as Cynthia described her frustration at the lack of assistance from the La Cresta police, Tamera winced, silently comparing the non-action of the local officers with that of their Australian counterparts in a television documentary she'd seen weeks before regarding a missing Sydney girl. From the moment the Australian police were contacted, they'd interviewed the missing girl's family members in separate rooms, thoroughly inspected her bedroom, bagged her toothbrush, comb, and hairbrush, dissected her garbage, questioned neighbours and friends, and mounted a physical search in the wooded area near to her home.

Cynthia only had her friends to rely on, and as far as Tamera was concerned, the police had in effect abandoned LaToya and her mother.

*Did someone take her? Is she being held against her will?* Tamera wasn't sure.

The candlelight vigil was held as planned on the open plot of land at the corner of Chester Street, and in the coming days, volunteers distributed flyers throughout La Cresta and the neighbouring towns. Friends and family members affixed posters to utility poles, bus stalls, banks, grocery stores, restaurants, and other areas where they could be easily seen by the public. Tamera and her friends uploaded several photos of LaToya to their Facebook pages, circulating them to everyone they could think of. Her image was also distributed to the local media, and several days after her disappearance, almost every resident of La Cresta watched the seven o'clock news when Cynthia was interviewed.

Exactly one week after LaToya vanished, two elementary school boys playing hide-and-seek with their friends smelled a foul odour deep inside a bushy area on the unoccupied plot of land at Chester Street. The told their parents and Joshua, Charlie, Earl, and Renwick volunteered to search the grounds, banking on it being a false alarm.

"This shouldn't take us too long." Joshua stood at the edge of the unfenced property with the others. They couldn't smell anything, but as they ventured into the thick brush, the wind blew the faint smell of death toward them.

"Let's check over there," Charlie said. The men gnawed through the heavy bush with their cutlasses.

"Over there." Earl pointed. They covered their noses, looking down at the remains of a worm- and fly-infested corpse.

"It's only a big dog," Renwick said.

Despite the collective efforts of the community, one week stretched to two, and still no one was closer to finding LaToya.

# 5.

"I'M SO GLAD CASSANDRA WON the calypso monarch title again," Jan said as she and Tamera turned onto Chester Street. They were wearing white T-shirts and black shorts, and they had red, white, and gold glitter sprinkled all over their faces. They also carried wings covered in bright purple fabric, and gold-and-green headpieces. Their class had placed second at the costume competition, but none of their classmates could, in all honesty, complain because the general consensus at school was that the winners deserved it.

"I still can't believe that Delroy didn't win the King of Carnival prize," Tamera said.

"Did you see Mr. Samuel's face when Delroy got second place?"

"Yeah," Tamera said. "I've never seen such a large frown on him."

They walked hurriedly past Edgar and Samuel's homes. The girls didn't want to run into Edgar. The brothers had fallen out during the past week, and Edgar, a skilled carpenter when he wasn't drinking, was constructing a wall to separate his property from his brother's.

Days earlier, Samuel had confided in Earl that Edgar's alcoholism had worsened and that he was becoming belligerent. "Imagine, he came to my house as drunk as a fish and disrespected my family. When I told him about it he got more angry than me, and that's why he's building that sky-high barricade to block me out. As far as I'm concerned he's not a member of my family no more."

Tamera's cell phone rang as she and Jan crossed the street in front of Edgar's half-finished wall. Even before checking the caller ID, Tamera knew the call was from Dalton. That Saturday, because of his work commitments, Dalton wasn't able to return to the village to attend the school carnival celebrations. At eighteen, he was one and a half years older than Tamera, having graduated from secondary school the previous June. He'd never missed the school carnival show during the five years he was enrolled as a student, and during his final year he participated in the King of Carnival competition for the first time, placing third.

He usually phoned Tamera at about eight o'clock almost every evening, but he had told her ahead of time that he was going to contact her earlier so she could share the results of the various carnival competitions at her school.

"It's good to know that everything went well," he said. "Sorry I had to miss it this year."

"Yeah, it was really good, except that LaToya's still on everybody's minds," Tamera said. "It's horrible that we don't know what happened to her, and a lot of people are still thinking that she ran away with somebody. Her mother's at home worried sick, and I'm feeling guilty that we were at school celebrating."

"You can't stop living because someone's missing," Dalton said. "The reality is that over half a dozen missing people are still unaccounted for in Juniper and Toledo this year alone, so if we stop enjoying life because a person vanishes, then we will be miserable all the time."

"But it's different when you know the person," Tamera sighed. "Me and LaToya aren't best friends, but she is a decent person, and it's real scary that someone disappeared from a tiny place like this and nobody don't know nothing."

"I know what you mean," he said. "LaToya's mother lives next door to my family, and I'm sorry about what happened to her, but I have to live my life, and you have to live yours too."

Tamera waved Jan goodbye as she turned to toward her home, the phone still glued to her ear. Tamera remained on the porch and chatted with her long-distance boyfriend for another ten or fifteen minutes. When she entered the house, her father was sprawled on the recliner that he'd purchased for his wife's fortieth birthday the previous year. Earl, with a drink in hand, looked up at Tamera and gave her a crooked smile. A half-filled bottle of rum was on the floor next to the recliner, and a bottle of cola was next to it. "Your mother eyes were so full of fire when we met," he slurred, emptying the glass in his mouth.

"Ma's okay?" she asked as he poured another drink.

"She had big dreams," he sputtered, then choked as he slugged back the drink. When he stopped coughing, he started to cry.

Tamera had only seen her father cry once before, and that was on the day his mother died.

"Life can give you roses or thorns, and you have to deal with whatever comes your way. You have to make the best of the cards that you draw," he sputtered, and after gulping back another shot of rum, he placed the empty glass at his feet.

"I'm going to take a shower, Pa." Tamera didn't want to discuss her mother and needed to escape her father's presence.

"You can't spare your old man a few minutes?" he whined.

"Sure, Pa, but just let me wash off this gunk first." She returned moments later with a bare face and some clean clothes, and reluctantly settled on the sofa facing him.

"When I asked your mother to marry me, she said no the first time, but I didn't give up that easily, and she agreed to be my wife when I proposed the second time." Earl had shared this tale many times before, but Tamera remained silent. She nodded and let him continue with his story.

After listening to her dad ramble for over fifteen minutes, she couldn't get her mother out of her mind. She thought of the previous November when Alison had been discharged from the hospital and how quickly after returning home her mood had begun to fluctuate. Some days she was on a high and on other days she sank really low. At times, she had more energy than a two-year-old and she and her sister couldn't keep up with her. During those times, she acted all-powerful and invincible, operating on less than three hours sleep a day. She painted watercolours for hours as if she had a pressing deadline. Her paintings were mediocre at best, yet she tried to convince her husband and kids that they'd sell for millions. It was during those times that Tamera almost wished her mother would get back to being down; it was so much easier to be with her when her mood was low. They could at least keep her still in one place. When she was high, there was no stopping her, and the whole family would have to be on high alert. Anything could happen.

The following Saturday, Mary and Tamera accompanied their father to the hospital to visit their mother. Children under twelve weren't allowed to set foot in the institution, so Renwick stayed at home with Emma. Uneasy, Tamera stepped through the door, spotting her mother among the inpatients, many of whom had an empty, spaced-out look. Compared to the sparkling sunshine they'd left outside moments earlier, the dull and dim space inside the hospital felt stuffy and stale. Alison sat quietly on a chair, rubbing her lower arm mechanically. Several women in the gloomy room were making large, jerky movements and chattering incessantly under their breaths. Alison must have noticed her family members as they came through the door, because that very moment she slid out of her seat and came forward to greet them with short laboured steps. They met in the middle of the large room and she pawed at their sleeves as they encircled her.

"Hi, Ma." Mary hugged her. "How are you?"

"Good," she said.

"We brought you this." Tamera held up a basket full of ripe fruit.

"You have more than enough to last the entire week," Earl said with a gentle smile.

"Any Julie mangoes in there?" she said, peeking.

"Of course, Ma," Mary said, hugging her. "We know they're your favourite."

"Thanks for coming." Alison said, but she wasn't smiling and her tone lacked inflection.

The mangoes, sapodillas, and bananas in the fruit basket had been harvested from Pa's garden that morning; the apples and pears were purchased from a vendor in the vicinity of the hospital.

When the bell rang, signalling the end of visiting hours, a sudden gloominess appeared in Earl's eyes, and Tamera felt tightness in her stomach. She needed to take one last look at her mother before stepping out of the enclosed area, so she spun around at the door, keeping her eyes on her mom as she torturously stepped away, widening the space between them. She tottered like an elderly person and then sluggishly sank in a low-slung chair that faced the window. Tamera waved, but her mother didn't notice.

# 6.

T HE OFFICIAL CARNIVAL WEEKEND, a significant event on the island, arrived almost as quickly as Usain Bolt takes to hit the tape during a hundred-metre race. Tamera wasn't ecstatic simply because she had a four-day weekend, or that her cousin, Azura, had convinced her dad to make the long drive to the countryside to meet her so that she could enjoy the carnival festivities with close relatives. She was also overjoyed because Dalton was scheduled to return home that Friday evening. They planned to have a quick dip on Saturday morning with their closest friends, and later that afternoon, after relaxing at the beach, they were going to gather at Jan's house.

Tamera's Friday and Saturday plans went off without a hitch. But on Sunday, Uncle Richard and his daughter, Azura, didn't arrive at the house at half past ten as they were supposed to. Tamera tried to reach Azura on her cell phone, but all of her calls went directly to voicemail. She panicked because she didn't have her uncle's number, and before heading out that morning Earl had absentmindedly left his phone on the table, so Tamera couldn't reach him to get her uncle's phone number, nor did she know her dad's password to try and find her uncle's number on his phone.

Azura finally arrived at eleven thirty. "My phone died, and traffic was backed up for miles 'cause of a stupid accident, and to make matters worse, Dad's phone battery died," she moaned. "We've gotta rush, but I need to say hi to Mary and the baby first."

"They're not here," Tamera said. "They went to church."

"Church?" Azura's facial muscles tightened. "Since when does Mary go to church?"

Tamera shrugged and followed Azura to Uncle Richard's Pontiac Firebird. It was bright red and Tamera loved it.

"All set?" Richard said, clutching the steering wheel.

"Yes, Uncle," Tamera said and climbed into the idling vehicle with a wide smile, dumping her duffle bag onto the vacant space next to her.

"You're coming up here during the Easter holidays?" Tamera asked, turning to face Azura. "Uncle Charlie's invited both of us to go with him and Jan to see the leatherback turtles lay their eggs."

"I'm definitely coming," Azura said. "I can hardly wait to see the turtles in action."

Richard's car rounded the corner, quickly approaching Dalton's parents' home where the lone cashew tree swayed in the strong breeze. On the opposite side of the street, a carload of people entered the white house covered with flowering bushes. "That's LaToya's place," Tamera said, pointing. People were still visiting Cynthia in droves.

"There's still no news about what happened to her?" Azura asked.

"No," Tamera said. "No one knows anything."

The carnival festivities ended and the weather remained humid and dry. The dense bush that had grown all over La Cresta during the previous months lost some of its opulence, a dull chestnut hue replacing its earlier emerald shimmer. But several days before Easter, the sky opened, and it resulted in mass flooding in low-lying areas. Azura climbed up the staircase to her Uncle Earl's home under the heavy downpour and slipped out of her squishy runners and wet sweater at the door. Her father darted in behind her, shedding his soaked sandals at the front door.

"You brought this never-ending rain from San Juan!" Charlie boomed at his brother, Earl, on the sofa. He had the deepest voice of all his siblings, despite his diminutive size. He wasn't just the shortest among them, but the leanest too. Since his separation from Jan's mother, he often visited his brother's home on weekends and sometimes in the evenings as well. He and Earl also often talked in private, and they'd usually stop in midsentence if by chance anyone walked into the room.

For the first time since her parents' separation, Jan had gone to the city to spend some quality time with her mother. She'd been in Port City for almost a week and was scheduled to return home the night before the trip they had planned with her father and cousins to see the leatherback turtles lay their eggs.

"Tammy, bring three glasses, a beer for your Uncle Charlie, and a bottle of water from the fridge." Earl pulled out a half-empty flask of rum from one of the kitchen cupboards and dropped it on the coffee table in front of his brothers. Tamera did as her father requested. He and Richard filled their glasses with a generous amount of liquor, swallowing it in one shot, after which they chased it down with cold glasses of water. Charlie savoured a Carib beer, and when he was done he requested another. For a while, Tamera's two uncles and father reminisced about their boyhood days, smacking each other on the shoulder every time they remembered something funny or unusual. Tamera thought they were hilarious.

"You're still trying to sell that piece of land?" Richard suddenly asked.

"Yeah," Earl said. "But so far nobody's offering me what it's worth."

"If you'd taken my advice and put it in an agent's hand, then you would have already found a buyer," Charlie said, trying to sound authoritative.

"There's no guarantee 'bout that," Earl said curtly. Tamera knew he wanted his brother to stay out of it.

"Don't let us fight," Richard said. "But my advice to you, brother, is to spend a few dollars and advertise in the daily newspaper, and the right buyer will eventually come along."

Earl was the eldest among his siblings and had taken care of his parents as they had aged. He had inherited four plots of land from them; only one plot each had been bequeathed to Charlie and Richard. Richard had sold his plot of land before relocating to San Juan.

"Is the first of May suitable for all of you?" Earl asked as he and his brothers tried to choose a date for the annual family gathering, customarily held at Earl's home. At these traditional family gatherings, Tamera's uncles usually assisted with the food preparations. They passed the rest of the afternoon discussing what they would prepare for that day, and how.

The menu often included *buljol*, one of Earl's favourite dishes made with shredded salt codfish. He enjoyed combining *buljol* with coconut bakes, a coconut bread made with wheat flour, coconut flakes, and coconut oil. Additionally, the family usually prepared stewed fish, baked fish, some plain rice, a mixed green salad, coleslaw, and a variety of local vegetables including avocado and fried plantains.

"It's always fish, fish and more fish," Azura grumbled as her dad and uncles revealed their chosen menu.

When they had finished ironing out all the details, Earl followed Richard to the porch, and for a few minutes they had a private conversation. Tamara often wondered what they would say to each other in those moments. It always looked so serious. Afterward, Richard bounded to his car, using an old newspaper to shelter him from the unyielding rainstorm. Charlie jumped off the sofa and made his way home about half an hour later.

The inclement weather refused to relent, so with nothing better to do, Azura accompanied Tamera to her room. She settled on Tamera's queen-sized bed, switched on her tablet, and surfed the 'net. Tamera booted up her computer and played her favourite online typing game. About an hour later, a glow brightened the room, followed by booming thunder. Then the computer screen went dark.

"I guess that's the end of my game until the power returns," Tamera moaned.

"I can at least read a book," Azura said and fired up the Kindle software on her tablet. But barely half an hour later, she sighed. "Gosh! I forgot to charge my battery last night, and now it's dead." She abandoned her tablet on the middle of Tamera's bed and walked out of the bedroom.

"I'm real sorry," Tamera said, following her elder cousin to the living room.

"It's nobody's fault that it's raining or that the power's gone," Azura said.

"The stormy weather surely caused the outage," Earl said, sitting on his wife's recliner, and sticking his neck out from behind a newspaper. Azura plopped onto the couch then tapped her toes and drummed her fingers, breaking the silence in the living room. Tamera tried to initiate a conversation, but Azura yawned in the middle of each brief response to Tamera's questions. She gradually fell asleep on the sofa, and Tamera felt as if her head would burst from boredom.

The extraordinary time Tamera had shared with Azura while visiting her in San Juan during the carnival celebrations was fresh in Tamera's memory, and she was mortified at not being able to offer Azura a similar experience. Besides taking in the parade of the bands on Carnival Tuesday with Azura's family, Tamera had also attended several events with her relatives including the J'ouvert celebrations that started at four on Carnival Monday morning and marked the official start of the two-day carnival celebrations; the calypso tent that feautured performances by a number of calypso bands and soca musicians throughout the festival; and the Dimanche Gras show, where individuals compete for the Calypso Monarch crown, and men and women in elaborate costumes vie for the King and Queen of Carnival titles.

Tamera stared dolefully out the window at the sheets of rain that poured down, thinking about the plans she and her friends had made and that had had to be cancelled.

At five, a call came in on Azura's mobile. She leapt off the sofa, and slipped into Tamera's bedroom for privacy. Earl and Tamera had settled around the dining table with a deck of cards and passed the time playing "go to pack" under candlelight. Azura came out of the bedroom exuding a much sunnier spirit than when she'd entered. By then the small hand on the wall clock was pointing to six. Tamera sighed. The time seemed to be inching by.

"The power's back!" Tamera cried out as the room was illuminated, but the heavy rain had tapered off only marginally.

"You want to watch anything special?" Earl asked Azura as she removed the remote from the sofa and placed it on the centre table next to her cell phone; she settled in a chair where the remote had been, next to her uncle.

"Not really." She shifted on the chair, trying to make herself comfortable as she tucked her legs beneath her, and then pulled her phone into her lap.

Earl switched on the television and flicked through the channels. "Let's see what's happening in the local news today."

A man who looked quite a bit older than Earl and was dressed in a checkered, short-sleeved shirt and rolled up khaki pants grimaced as he faced the camera. His eyes narrowed as he spoke. "Fishermen today have it much harder than when I started going out on the water with my father," the man said. "We use to catch close to five hundred carite, salmon, and kingfish a day, and on the odd occasion when we caught less than half of that, we would consider it a terrible day. Nowadays, if we manage to catch two hundred and fifty fish we're more than satisfied."

"Why do you think the catch is less than before?" a youthful reporter asked the man.

"Pollution," he said. "It's plain pollution. "People on pleasure crafts and people living too close to the shore contaminating the water."

"How are they polluting it?"

"People dump their waste," he said. "The owners of pleasure crafts are among the main culprits because they dump their sewage in the sea too, and this creates E.coli in the water. If you take the time to observe, you'll notice that the water is whitish at times, with a greenish tinge. That is the algae. It uses up the oxygen, and the fish are struggling. And to make matters worse, for the past month the water has been unusually rough, and this often makes our job too treacherous."

"Do you want to add anything to what your colleague has stated?" the reporter asked a nearby man with unusually large shoulders and arms.

"Yeah," the man said with a serious expression. "We used to have a lot of mangrove. They cut down a lot of it, and bait no longer comes to shore. Most of our fishing is done with live bait, and the problem could easily be fixed by placing used tires to create an artificial reef. In no time it would help to increase the food chain."

"Anything else?" the reporter asked a third man.

"Another problem is that the banks are not using boats as security, nor are they accepting houses or land, so if we don't have cash or shares in a financial institution, we can't get even a small loan to repair our vehicles. And we need to pay our bills just like everyone else."

"Do lots of pleasure craft come down here?" Azura asked her uncle when the news went to commercial.

"Very rarely do we see them down these parts," he said. "But our catch is also affected by people who live close to the water and indiscriminately dump their garbage in the sea. We don't want no pleasure boats to further hamper our livelihood, so we're thankful that they hardly ever roam 'bout these parts."

"It must be really hard to be a fisherman," she said. "My dad often talks about the days when as a boy he used to go fishing with his dad."

"Those were the good old days," Earl said. "I loved every moment of it, but your dad hated it."

"I know," she said. "Dad told me that as soon as he finished school, he moved closer to the city 'cause he wanted to escape having to go fishing with his dad. He's not an outdoor person at all."

"That's Richard, your father," Earl said. "But for me, even though this job has some major challenges, I have no regrets. The fishermen down here have a lot to thank God for because we can still make a half-decent living compared to folks elsewhere."

"Do the fishermen here have problems getting loans too?" Azura asked.

"Yeah, the same rules apply on the entire island, but whenever possible I make sure to put some money aside for emergency situations."

"It never crossed my mind before that those pleasure craft caused so much pollution," Azura said.

"Me either," said Tamera, leaning forward and listening attentively to everything her father was explaining to them.

"That's why we don't want developers here," he said. "The huge piece of land where the youngsters sometimes play ball could go to a developer at any time, and my fear is if that happens it could possibly be converted into a resort. We don't want that kind of thing here, but who knows what will happen in the next few years. Life is full of changes. My hope is that no major changes happen in this community until after I'm gone."

"But," Azura said, "wouldn't a resort create jobs for the locals?"

"Yeah, but at what cost?" he said. "It might provide jobs,

but it could also unleash a whole host of new problems in this small village."

"Pa," Tamera interrupted, "can you take me and Azura fishing with you one day this week?"

"Azura's just like her dad," he said. "She may not want to do that."

"I don't mind trying it once," Azura said, smiling agreeably.

Tamera's jaw fell open. Azura beamed.

# 7.

EARL'S FIBREGLASS BOAT WAS SIMPLE and open, and all of his net-hauling was done by hand. Renwick and his brother, Clyde, usually prepared the fishing net before it was time to head out to sea. The three men routinely boarded the vessel at around four or five in the afternoon and typically returned between six and eight the following morning. Most of their catch was sold wholesale to a particular commercial buyer, but a quota was set aside for purchase by the residents of La Cresta.

Earl followed his usual routine on the day his niece and daughter headed to the dock with him. Tamera was an old hand at fishing, so for her it was just another day of business. When Mary and Tamera were younger, Earl often took them out to sea. But those trips ended after Mary had her baby and Alison's health began to deteriorate. When that happened, Tamera began to spend large blocks of time away from home, liming with Jan and her friends at the beach or at Jan's parents' home. At times, Tamera remained a recluse in her bedroom, where she occupied herself by playing computer games and talking to her friends on the phone or through social media. She also slept abnormally long hours. All in all, while at home, Tamera hardly interacted with anyone, preferring the company of her friends to the exclusion of everyone else.

"I can't believe you haven't gone fishing before," Tamera said to Azura as they stepped out of Earl's vehicle at the docking port, where at least twenty fishing boats were anchored. There were seven crudely built wooden storage sheds and two mending sheds within close proximity to the shore.

"I didn't say that I haven't ever gone fishing," she replied. "What I said is that I haven't fished from a boat before, but I've fished many times from the bank of the river."

"It's not the same," Tamera assured her.

Earl's red, green, and gold pirogue was anchored among a host of colourful vessels, almost all of which were open like his, but a few were partially covered. A handful of fishermen and one fisherwoman had already boarded their boats, but many others, including Earl and his assistants, were still preparing their supplies for the journey at sea. Some folks were checking their nets while others were preparing their bait. Four men with wrinkled faces from years of facing the elements were settled on a bench under a tent playing cards, a dilapidated greenish table positioned in front of them. The only bald man among the four slapped a card face up on the half-broken table.

"Got you!" The man grinned. Another man grunted, but Tamera couldn't see his face.

"One more time!" the bald man yelled melodically, bundling the deck of cards and shuffling them like a professional gambler. Meanwhile, another group of men lazed around, idly watching the comings and goings at the dock.

"They're waiting for boats that have already gone out to return with their catch," Clyde said when Azura asked why those men were sitting by the jetty. "Fishermen will go out in the day or night depending on the type of fish they want to catch."

Earl's face stiffened; he mumbled softly to Renwick, and together they stepped toward a quiet spot a fair distance from everyone. He lifted his right arm and wagged his index finger. He rattled on, and Renwick, with a disconcerted expression, kept his eyes on his father-in-law's face, but his lips didn't move. Renwick then shifted slightly and shook his head as if denying an allegation. Earl's arms slipped to his side, and he listened in silence as Renwick seemed to be explaining his position. Tamera's eyes strayed from Renwick and Earl to a tall, broad-shouldered man who was labouring over a pirogue the same size as her dad's but with a more subdued design.

"Your father looks really upset," Azura commented as she stared intently at her uncle and Renwick.

"Pa always talks down to him 'cause he acts like an idiot at times," Tamera replied. "That's nothing new, believe me."

Clyde gathered the supplies, and Earl and Renwick made their way toward Tamera and Azura, their faces surprisingly relaxed despite their earlier heated exchange.

"You're ready to hit the water?" Earl winked.

"Yeah, I'm totally ready," Azura said boldly, standing next to Tamera and giving her a high-five. Azura looked very smart in her red T-shirt and red-and-white shorts with black running shoes and matching black socks turned down. Next to her, Tamera felt she looked shabby in her old, torn jeans and white tank top.

"Well, we'd better get going." Earl ordered Renwick and Clyde to carry the supplies to the boat and motioned for the girls to follow.

Azura hesitated. "It's okay," Clyde said. "Follow me."

"I'd rather get on that wooden boat close to the shore and then hop on," Azura explained.

"Not a problem," Clyde said as a tall man, a friend of Earl's, climbed into the boat.

"Bossman, me and the young ladies coming aboard to get to Mr. Telford's vessel," Clyde said to Christopher George, whose son was one of Tamera's classmates.

"No problem," Mr. George gestured with his hand for them to hop aboard.

Clyde looked at Azura. "Let me go first, and then I'm going to help you on."

"Okay," she nodded, relieved to have some help.

Clyde boarded the wooden vessel and tipped forward, offering Azura his hand. She grasped his palm, stretching her long limbs to climb over the sides and into the boat As she spun around on the wooden boat admiring her surroundings, Clyde offered Tamera his hand as well.

Tamera shook her head. "I'm going to walk through the water to get to Pa's boat," she said.

Azura followed Clyde to the edge of the boat closest to where Earl's vessel was anchored. He hopped onto Earl's vessel and helped Azura over. Tamera took off her sandals, clutching them in one hand, and waded through the ankle-deep water. The boat swayed as she leapt on. Her father and Renwick boarded right after.

The vessel moved off quickly, and Azura spread her arms to get her balance. As the pirogue glided into deeper water, she said, "The land's getting lower and the water so much higher." Eventually the land disappeared completely, and they were surrounded by the enormous, glimmering sea.

Earl kept his boat closer to the shore or steered it farther out to sea, depending on the type of fish he was seeking. He used rectangular mesh nets with floats that were strung in a line and glowed in the dark. The size of the net hinged on the type of fish he wanted to catch. The boat had a sizeable refrigerator where the fish were stored. He didn't fish for crabs or lobsters, but his colleagues who did used wire traps for that.

Renwick liked to fish with the radio on. He didn't play it too loud, but the volume was just high enough that everyone aboard could enjoy the music. Azura and Clyde rattled on, even when it was Clyde's turn to monitor the nets. Machel Montano's "Whistle and Wine" song came on and all chatter ended as Azura abruptly burst into song.

"I'm going to be sick." Her face lost its colour halfway through her performance; she spread her fingers over her chest and tipped her head.

"Here, hold this," Clyde said and handed her a plastic bag. "Urg." Her face tensed, as she emptied her stomach into it. Clyde offered her a bottle of water, and Earl and Renwick monitored their surroundings. "Come on, man, it's time to help us pull up the net," Earl said. His and Clyde's eyes collided.

"Okay, bossman." Clyde stepped toward Earl, and the three men jerked the weighty net closer to them. Along with the fish they'd targeted, some unintentional catch was strewn at their feet.

"You need to come out to sea more often," Tamera said, staring at Azura's face that was as white as a ghost's. "You'll get used to it."

"We're going to head back to shore," Earl suddenly announced. Tamera scowled. And even though her father didn't specifically admit to it, she guessed that he'd elected to cut the trip short because Azura's motion sickness wasn't letting up.

Renwick was the first to notice that the float on the illuminating gillnets had balled up and was no longer strung in a line. "There's lots of twisting going on," Earl said as a large turtle's head came up and gasped for air. They could see immediately that it was badly tangled in the net.

"Why one of you don't dive in and free the poor animal?" Azura seemed to have mysteriously recovered, looking extremely perturbed at the turtle's predicament.

"You must be crazy," Renwick said. "You want us to risk our lives for a reptile?"

"It didn't ask to be caught. It needs our help," she insisted.

"Anyway, we're on our way back," Renwick said. "They can hold their breath for close to an hour."

"You can't do that," she said, " 'cause it took us hours to get here, and it's going to take as long for us to get back."

"We're going to pull in the net right now." Clyde smiled, stepping closer to the back of the boat where the net was attached. "Renwick's just pulling your leg."

The turtle came up, again gasping for air, its flippers flailing violently enough to break a man's arms. "We're going to try our best to free him," Earl said.

"Stop fighting. We can't help you if you don't keep calm." Clyde's voice rose, and his face tensed as he prepared to slit the net to free the animal. He nipped it slightly, and the creature maneuvered its limbs as if it were fighting off a lion. Then, the turtle beat the water with its strong flippers, splashing salt water all over them.

"You're not giving us no choice." Earl rushed to aid Clyde, who'd almost fallen overboard.

"It's real tricky to free a fighting eight-hundred-pound turtle that's acting as if it's crazy," Earl said as Clyde steadied himself. The turtle twisted and turned over and over again, causing seawater to splash on the vessel and the boat to bounce violently over the swells. Earl grabbed a stick, angling his body toward the aggressive turtle; he aimed for the tiny white spot on the creature's head. "Woop!"

Tamera covered her eyes with both hands, sparing herself from witnessing the aftereffects. "It didn't give me no choice," Earl said. "We have to be careful not to get caught in the net while trying to free these powerful creatures. If we're careless, we could all end up at the bottom of the sea."

"All that turtle meat's going to waste?" Renwick grimaced after his father-in-law released the reptile's carcass into the sea.

"You murdered that turtle!" Azura screamed, glaring at the entire crew. It took almost ten minutes for Earl to calm her down. Tamera also felt sick to her stomach, but she understood why her father had to do what he did. There was nothing else that could have been done.

She put her arm around Azura's shoulders. "We tried," she said softly.

"It's going to be costly to repair this net again," Earl moaned.

"Those nets aren't good for the animals. They cause thousands of turtles to die each year," Clyde said under his breath. Motioning to Renwick, he started to pack the fish they'd caught in the large rectangular refrigerator at the back of the boat. Renwick joined him and together they finished the job.

There were no winners. Earl and his colleagues needed to support their families, and Tamera couldn't deny that the use of the gill nets caused many turtles to die, so on their way home, she didn't say anything else, and only turned a couple of times to pat Azura's arm.

When they returned to land, Earl sold three quarters of his catch to a wholesale merchant who collected the fish in a white van; the rest was earmarked for the locals.

"I'm going to talk to Micky 'bout repairing this net," Earl said. "It's a big hassle, 'cause I already spent thousands of dollars on repairs this year," he added, shaking his head. "Renwick's going to take you girls straight home."

Tamera and Azura followed Renwick to his vehicle and Earl and Clyde walked in the opposite direction, approaching the mending sheds.

"I once read that over three thousand leatherbacks are tangled in nets every year, but I never thought I'd see one being killed with my own eyes," Azura said as she and Tamera climbed into Renwick's vehicle.

No one spoke, and the next thing Tamera heard was Renwick's voice. "We're home," he said. "Wake up and stop snoring."

# 8.

J AN RETURNED FROM HER MOTHER'S Port City residence the evening before her dad planned to take her and her cousins to the beach where the leatherback turtles laid their eggs. She dumped her luggage on her bedroom floor and rushed to Uncle Earl's house, joining Azura and Tamera on the porch. "You guys heard that the police found the body of the missing San Pedro girl?" Jan said.

"No," Tamara said.

"I didn't hear anything either," Azura said.

"They found her body in some bushes close to the Carson River," Jan said. "I heard it on the news in Dad's car when he was driving me home."

"Wow," Tamera said. "They arrested anyone?"

"Not yet," Jan said.

"That's really sad." Azura frowned.

Tamera scowled. "I hope the same thing didn't happen to LaToya."

"Of all the girls missing so far this year, they only found one body. All the others are still unaccounted for," Jan said.

"Sometimes I'm convinced there's human trafficking on this island," Azura said.

"You really think that?" Jan said, her eyes wide.

"Don't look at me as if I'm crazy," Azura said.

The following afternoon, Charlie tooted his horn several times, trying to round up the girls and get started on their trip.

"Azura!" Tamera rattled the handle on the bathroom door. "Uncle Charlie's ready to go."

"I'm coming." Azura said, sticking her neck out of the bathroom for a moment. Then she ducked back into the bathroom, this time leaving the door wide open.

"Hurry up!" Tamera said impatiently as she peered into the room to glare at her cousin, who was meticulously daubing on purple eyeshadow. "Uncle Charlie's going to leave us if we don't hurry."

"He wouldn't dare do that," Azura calmly replied, slipping a small bag containing her cosmetics inside her handbag. She stepped out of the house, her face beautifully done up.

When they got to the car, Azura shifted sideways, allowing Tamera to climb into their uncle's Subaru ahead of her. Jan was already in the back seat; Tamera shuffled in next to Jan, and Azura settled alongside her.

"Glad you could make the trip, girls, but it's lonely up here," Charlie said.

Azura and Tamera glanced at each other. "You're not gonna sit up front next to your dad?" Azura said, shifting her glance to Jan.

"I'm staying right here." Jan smiled.

"I'm going to sit up front then," Azura said.

"That's better," Charlie said when Azura slid into the seat next to him.

In addition to his keen interest in fitness, Charlie was also an avid nature lover who often hiked the myriad nature trails all over the island. The previous year, Tamera had travelled with him and his family to Smith's Nature Centre, an amazing resort buried deep in the mountainous rainforest. The year before they travelled to the hilly resort, they'd visited the famous Henry Swamp at the mouth of the country's largest river. The swamp is the home to one hundred species of birds including bananaquits, scarlet ibises, and herons. There they had boarded a small boat, and their guide navigated numerous channels where thick mangrove foliage hung suspended over their heads creating a verdant canopy that barely allowed the sun to stream through.

During their journey through the wetlands, Tamera was especially intrigued by the bright red big-beaked scarlet ibises flying overhead in a V-formation, their elegant necks outstretched. "They get their bright red colour by eating red shellfish rich in carotene," Charlie explained. "The young birds are born grey and white, and it takes roughly two years for them to get their red colour."

Charlie was a physical education teacher and had planned this trip to see the leatherbacks to coincide with the Easter school break. Most of his nature tours occurred when school was out, but at times he made weekend trips to various places. And he was always happy to bring his daughter and her cousins along for the fun.

It was the first time Tamera had been on a trip with Charlie and Jan in the absence of Jan's mother. From the moment she sat in the car and buckled her seat belt, she silently mourned her absence. Jan's mom had moved out of her family home about four months earlier, but Tamera felt as if she'd been gone much longer.

"I know the answer," Azura said in response to Charlie's question about how many eggs the leatherback turtles laid every year. "It's been estimated the females lay approximately fifteen thousand eggs every two years."

"How come you know so much about them?" Tamera asked as Azura rattled off all the facts she had learned about the giant reptiles.

"I did a school project about the leatherbacks last year, and I got the highest mark in my class," she boasted. "I can still see that poor creature gasping for air in Uncle Earl's net," she added, frowning.

"Those types of nets are a real hazard to the turtle population, and that's partly why these gentle creatures are endangered," Charlie said.

"Thank God we now have laws that prevent people from hunting them and eating their flesh," Azura added.

Tamera looked out the window, lost in thought while Charlie and Azura continued chatting. A million different things were going through her head: thoughts about Dalton and the photos he kept urging her to send, her anxiety about the upcoming end-of-school exams, worry over what happened to LaToya, and the dismal state of her mother's health. She was so engrossed she didn't hear a word of Charlie and Azura's conversation.

"Tammy? Tammy? You're okay?" Charlie asked, looking back at her with a bit of concern.

"Yeah, I'm cool," she replied, coming back to the present moment. She rolled her shoulders and sat up straight. The view outside her window was gorgeous and she focused on that.

"Good to know," Charlie nodded. "Jan?"

"She's sleeping," Tamera said, glancing over at her friend.

"Exams are fast approaching," Azura said. "I wish Dad would pay for me to go to the American University in Washington, D.C."

Charlie chuckled. "I don't think my brother has that kind of dough."

"I know," she replied. "But I wish we could afford it."

"What's wrong with the local schools?" Charlie asked.

"Nothing," Azura said, "but living on a little island can be so limiting."

"If you keep working as hard as you do, you could surely get an open scholarship," Charlie said. "You certainly have the potential."

"That's not an easy feat." Azura laughed nervously. "The competition is not just stiff at my school, but there are some really brilliant students at other schools who are vying for the scholarships as well. And there aren't that many to go around."

Tamera frowned. She didn't want to talk about school or

listen to a discussion on that topic. "How long before we get there?" she interrupted.

"Another hour or so," Charlie replied.

Unlike Azura, Tamera didn't have a clear path or goal regarding her future. Jan wasn't sure what she wanted to do in the future either, but her mom and dad were insisting that she go to university. Neither of Tamera's parents had ever put pressure on her to pursue higher education. The only thing she was sure she wanted in the future was to be Dalton's wife, but at sixteen she had a long wait ahead of her.

"Make sure you're making your own money before you marry anybody," Earl had advised his two daughters time and again. When Mary had told him she was going to marry Renwick, Tamera sensed that the reason he hadn't vehemently opposed the marriage was because Mary was already pregnant.

"We're going on a trip to one of the caves later this year. Everyone will have to be prepared to climb down a rope to get there," Charlie said, not hiding his excited at the prospect of this next adventure. "You're both coming?"

"No, thank you," Azura said.

"Well, if you change your mind we're going there sometime after the end of the school year, and you're invited."

"You're going, Tamera?" Azura asked.

"Of course."

"Your younger cousin's making you look like a scaredy-cat," Charlie laughed.

Tamera hadn't visited any of the caves on the island before, but Charlie had told his daughter and nieces about the length of rope needed to get to the base of one portion of the cave they were going to visit. He had been talking about this trip for some time and he always encouraged both of them to accompany him. He had also vividly described the sounds that poured out of the nearby underground river, and Tamera had often imagined herself on that trip with him. She couldn't wait and she said that to Azura.

"Sometimes I wonder if I really belong to this family," Azura chuckled. "You guys like all these weird things that I don't have any interest in."

"If you come, you might surprise yourself and enjoy it," Tamera said. Jan opened her eyes and blinked a couple of times, but she didn't speak.

Tamera's close friendship with Jan and Azura dated back to her earliest memories. Azura, at seventeen, was the most academically gifted of the three cousins. When she wrote the eleven-plus examination, she placed in the first fifteen out of almost twenty thousand students. She also succeeded at thirteen CSEC subjects, achieving twelve grade ones and one grade two.

When Azura was between the ages of six and twelve, she always spent the annual August holidays in La Cresta. During that time, she and her two younger cousins were inseparable, and the three of them would alternate nights between Tamera and Jan's homes. They shared everything and there was nothing that they didn't know about each other.

For the first time since the three girls had climbed into their uncle's vehicle, there was total silence. Charlie's eyes swept over them and he smiled affectionately.

They zipped past three white buildings located almost at the top of a very steep hill. "Girls," Charlie said, pointing out the window. "There's the government-owned housing development that's recently been on the news."

"You need an escalator to go up and down that mountain," Jan said.

"I heard that the apartments are rather small on the inside," Charlie said.

"The folks who live there must be packed in like sardines," Azura said, "just like the slave masters packed the boats during the Middle Passage."

"I'd hate to live in one of those," Tamera said. "I need to have my own yard where I can sit outside in the sun whenever I feel like it and be away from roaming eyes."

"Beggars can't be choosers," Charlie said. "If people want to have a big house, especially if they are born poor, then they must get a good education so they can finance it themselves."

After driving through a number of quiet village streets and down several winding roads, Charlie swerved around a tight corner, and ended up on a dirt road that lead to a large wrought iron gate. He'd made arrangements for them to spend the night at a guesthouse close to one of the beaches where the leatherbacks laid their eggs, and Tamera was excited about this new experience.

"We're here," Charlie said with a big grin, climbing out of the vehicle. "The beach we're heading to is protected during the leatherback nesting season, and everyone needs a permit, but don't worry, I've got ours right here." He patted the pocket on his shirt as he grabbed their bags from the trunk.

Pink and red bougainvillea and tall palm trees bordered the entrance leading to a long, octagonal wooden building. They walked through a massive gate, admiring the building that stood more than twenty feet above ground. Charlie and his daughter and nieces were led to a two-bedroom suite. The three girls occupied the larger bedroom with a queen-sized four-poster bed. Charlie carried his backpack to the smaller room next to a red clay-tiled bathroom.

After examining their sleeping quarters, they made their way to an open deck that was large enough for all of them to take in the sun and relax without feeling cramped.

"I could stay here for a month," Jan said, admiring the poui trees and an abundance of coconut, banana, and sugarcane in the distance. Soon the sun dimmed and twilight was upon them, accompanied by a warm and salty breeze from the nearby ocean.

Charlie arranged to have a guide, and while he talked to the man he'd hired to escort them to the beach, Tamera imagined she was a tourist just like the many foreigners who'd also made the journey to witness the leatherbacks lay their eggs. Their guide informed them that staff patrolling the beach would radio him as soon as they spotted the first turtle making its way up the shore. "It's time," their guide, a stocky man with a gummy smile, eventually said. There was almost no moonlight, so he gave Charlie a flashlight and held one himself. As they approached the beach, Charlie and the guide switched off their flashlights, and turned on smaller flashlights that shone a dim red light, which they were assured wouldn't affect the turtles.

"How long we're going to have to wait before we see one?" Tamera asked the guide as they got closer to the water.

"One's coming," he whispered.

Just then sand flew up in the air just ahead of them, and their guide pointed to the approaching turtle. Tamera's and her two cousins' eyes bulged as the gentle creature dragged its large frame up the sloping coastline, sweeping away the sand with its front flippers as it slowly inched forward. They remained a respectable distance away, and in next to no time, two others, their black shells glimmering, grunted as they lumbered up the beach. Each turtle was in a trancelike state as they found a spot they considered suitable for their purposes. Charlie and the girls watched entranced as each of the enormous reptiles meticulously excavated holes with their rear flippers.

A boy from another group stepped forward, gingerly touching an approximately seven-hundred-pound turtle; he snapped a photo. After laying their white eggs, the turtles carefully swept sand over their eggs with their front flippers to disguise the nesting spot. The girls were in awe as the turtles turned around and slowly headed back to the water.

"I think they lay about ninety eggs each time," Azura softly said.

"That's right," Charlie whispered. "We've just witnessed a ritual that has been carried on for millions of years."

There were more tourists than locals on the beach that night, and Tamera could tell because even those who were as brown as they were had mostly foreign accents. On the way back to their rooms, a teenage boy with an American accent approached Azura. "Hi, my name is Kyle," he said.

"I'm Azura," she replied, smiling.

"My parents were born here," Kye said, "but I was born and have lived in Boston my entire life." He introduced his parents, Michelle and Gerald Edwards, to Charlie and the girls, and Charlie invited the family of three to lime on the porch. Jan and Tamera paid special attention as Azura and Kyle chatted like old friends. Charlie and Kyle's parents talked too.

"This is our first visit in ten years," Michelle said.

"You must notice the way things have changed," Charlie said.

"Yes," Gerald said. "We knew things would be different, but we didn't think it would have changed so much in a decade."

"For the good or bad?" Charlie asked, learning forward in his chair.

"There's some good things, but we're disappointed about the rate of crime and the bureaucracy when doing business," Michelle said. "It can be frustrating."

"We've lived in the cold for twenty-five years, and as we get older we feel the need for warmer weather," Gerald said. "That's why we're looking to buy a piece of land in a quiet community where we can build a new home."

"We've had our fair share of winters, and the last one was worse than most," Michelle said. "I'd prefer our dream home to be within walking distance of the sea."

"My brother has a plot for sale that might interest you," Charlie said. "I can put you on to him if you like."

Jan and Tamera overheard snippets of the conversation between Azura and Kyle. They were mainly talking about school and his childhood in Boston. Suddenly their voices dropped so low that Jan and Tamera couldn't make out a single word. Azura and Kyle were looking at each other as if they were old friends who'd recently met after several years of forced separation. Eventually Jan and Tamera grew bored of trying to hear what the adults were talking about, so they retreated inside.

"You haven't told me anything about your visit with your mom," Tamera said. She and Jan were sprawled out on the four-poster bed.

"Well," Jan said. "Me and Mom spent a lot of time bonding."

"That's good."

"Yeah," she said. "She got her own place now and a new job too. She invited me to move in with her after exams."

"What are you going to do?"

"You bet I'm going to live with her."

"You think you're going to be happy living in the city?"

"I love living in the countryside, but I'd rather live in the city with my mother than remain here with Dad."

"Uncle Charlie's not going to be happy to hear that."

"You're not going to tell him, and I'm not going to tell him either, so he's not going to find out."

"You're going to still come up here to visit me, I hope."

"Of course," she said. "I'm going to come back to La Cresta pretty often."

"After completing the CSECs, you're going to have to switch to another school to study for the CAPE exam," Tamera said. "You know you gotta do that if you want to go to university."

"I know," Jan said. "But the program to study for the CAPE exam after the CSECs is only two years long. The good part is that I hope to get into one of the better high schools in the city, and that will also help me to prepare," Jan said. "I want both of my parents to be proud of me."

"You're always trying to please everybody. But I'm glad you're making this decision becaue it's going to make you happy for a change, and you're not just doing what your dad wants."

"I'm really happy now," Jan replied. "I beat myself up before I made my decision. But I know it's the right one, and the only thing left is to tell Dad I'm moving in with Mom."

"When are you going to do that?"

"I'm keeping my mouth shut until after exams. And you better, too!" Jan admonished.

"My lips are sealed," Tamera said and then slowly dozed off. Jan was fast asleep not long afterwards.

The next morning, Azura blushed as she told her two younger cousins about her long talk with Kyle, her new friend from Boston. If they hadn't known Azura all of their lives, based on her expression and tone of voice, they'd have believed she and Kyle were in a long-lasting romantic relationship. "Would you believe he applied to do his undergraduate studies at our local university?" Azura's eyes grew twice as big in a few seconds.

"Why would he want to go to university here?" Jan asked.

"I don't know." Azura shrugged. "Maybe he wants to be close to his parents."

"Or maybe he's cheap and doesn't want to pay the high fees that the schools in the States charge," Tamera giggled.

"What does it matter what his reason is?" Azura said. "If he comes to school down here, then me and him could see a lot of each other."

"What's your hunk of a boyfriend going to think if he could eavesdrop on this conversation?" Jan grinned.

"I'm not yet eighteen," Azura said. "Me and Andy are just good friends. I'm not in a rush to marry him or anybody else."

After breakfast, the girls got into Charlie's car, and as he steered the vehicle down the dirt road and back onto the paved street, Tamera thought about how some things had remained constant over the years, like the leatherback turtles that returned time and again to the same tropical beach of their birth to lay the eggs of the next generation. She reminisced about some of the changes she'd witnessed during her lifetime, and a wave of uneasiness hit her when she thought about the recent changes that were speeding up around her. Mary would soon have a brand new baby. Azura was heading off to university. Jan was going to live with her mom in the city and in less than six months would enrol at a new school, while she would soon be out of school with no plans in sight for the future.

*What will I do next?* Tamera cringed at the thought of her two favourite cousins moving ahead and leaving her behind.

# 9.

ALISON WAS DUE TO LEAVE the hospital on the same day Azura planned to return to her San Juan home. The previous day, Azura and Tamera had made a huge red, green, and gold poster, and hung it on the outside of Tamera parents' bedroom door. "*Welcome Home, Ma*," read the large, rectangular sign.

Tamera was relieved that her mother was coming home and that she and her family would no longer have to make regular trips to the hospital in Port City, but tangled among her feeling of elation was also intense fear. *Will she suffer another relapse?*

Tamera hated the ambience of the hospital, but it wasn't the main reason she hated to set foot in that institution. More than anything else, she was worried that if she got too close to her mother, she'd soon fall ill again. As though she was somehow at the root of her mother's illness. Tamera didn't share her confused feelings with her father, because she knew he wouldn't be able to make sense of them, but she couldn't shake her sense of somehow being at fault. She reluctantly sat in the back seat of the car with her eyes closed, her stomach as heavy as if she'd consumed a bowlful of tiny stones.

A picture of Alison in her younger and healthier days popped into Tamera's head. This image was abruptly replaced by one of her darting naked toward the door and her two daughters blocking her from going outside.

*Will it be weeks or months before her symptoms return?*
Azura sat up front with her uncle, chatting all the way to
San Juan. "See you at the family get-together," she said and
got out of the vehicle, her smile as bright as the sun.

"See you then," Tamera said. Azura waved, disappearing
inside her parents' house.

"I'm not a taxi driver," Earl said and refused to move the car.

"Why do you and Uncle Charlie have a phobia 'bout sitting
alone up front?" Tamera asked with a big sigh, as opened the
door and slid out the back seat.

"Because we're brothers."

"But you and Uncle Charlie are different in almost every
other way," she said, settling next to Earl. "He keeps fit all the
time, and you never ever do any exercise. He loves exploring
nature, and you don't."

"I may not be as obsessed as my brother about going on those
nature trips, but as far as exercise goes, I do backbreaking
work on both sea and land," Earl replied. "Your uncle simply
orders kids around during his physical education classes. He
doesn't have as strenuous a job as mine." Earl turned on the
radio, and Tamera dozed off as soft music wafted around
her. Half asleep, she thought about a time long ago when
her mother was well enough to help her father harvest the
crops and mend the fishing nets. They would work side by
side, almost in rhythm, often laughing as they worked. They
were happier times.

"We're here," her father said and tapped her arm to wake her.

"Already?" She squinted in the sunlight.

As they entered the hospital, the weight on her chest felt like
a ton of bricks.

*Maybe Ma's cured, and she'll never act crazy again.* Tamera
repeated those words over and over again in her head, even
though she didn't believe them. She slowed her pace, allowing
her father to step ahead.

Mary had remained at home and was preparing her mom's

favourite dish. She'd seasoned the goat the previous afternoon, and the pot was already on the fire by the time Earl and Tamera headed out the door that morning.

*Ma will enjoy her meal when she gets home,* Tamera thought as she followed her father through the dull brown door.

"How are you doing?" Earl leaned forward and hugged his wife where she sat in a chair by the bed.

Tamera stood next to her mother and leaned down to place a kiss on her cheek.

"Good," Alison replied, looking around her and past Earl to see if anyone else was there. "Where's Mary?" she asked.

"She's at home cooking your favourite meal," Tamera said.

"Curried goat?"

"Yeah, Ma."

"That's nice to hear," Alison said, smiling brightly.

"We're ready to take you home," Earl said, gathering his wife's bags.

"I'm real happy to sleep in my own bed tonight," Alison said as she rose from her chair and tried to help Earl.

Tamera sighed with relief. Alison no longer had that demented look, and Tamera felt as if her real mother was finally back.

*Don't get your hopes up too high,* a voice whispered inside her head, and the negative thoughts that had momentarily seeped out of Tamera's mind returned.

After her return, Tamera doted on her mother. She didn't want to lose her mother again, so she tried harder than ever to please her. Tamera believed that the less stress Alison endured, the better her chances of remaining stable and well. So days later, when Tamera's school friends decided to lime at the beach, she shook her head and said, "Ma needs me. I can't go." Instead, she would race home after school to check on her and see if she needed anything. Often she would bring her a snack and a cup of tea, then sit at her feet and talk to her about the day at school.

A week later, Charlie accompanied the parents of the boy who had befriended Azura at the beach to Earl's front door.

"These are the folks who're interested in seeing the land," Charlie said after he had introduced Gerald and Michelle Edwards to Earl.

"Nice that you could make it." Earl shook their hands. "Let me show you around."

He slipped on his shoes and followed the couple and Charlie down the staircase. He led them toward the side of the house and over to the plot of land that was for sale.

Tamera watched them with avid interest then ran into the house to phone Azura "You remember that guy you met on the beach?" Tamera was breathless but held the phone firmly, waiting for Azura to respond.

"Who? Kyle?"

"Yes, him."

"What about him?"

"His parents are looking at the land Pa has for sale right now." Tamera was grinning from ear to ear, picturing the look on Azura's face as she heard this news.

"They are?"

"Yep."

"That's cool!"

"Do you still keep in touch with him?" Tamera asked.

"Yeah," she said, "by email, but it's just a casual thing."

"I'm going to keep you posted of any developments," Tamera said.

After viewing the property, the couple drove off in a rental car. "I think there's a very good chance they're going to make an offer." Charlie sounded upbeat as he and Earl made their way back to the living room.

"They surely seemed interested," Earl said, and with a wide grin, he offered his brother a beer.

# 10.

LIFE SEEMED ALMOST PERFECT the day before the annual family get-together at Tamera's parents' house. Her mother was still well and her father appeared happier than he'd been in months. Mary and Renwick hadn't bickered for weeks and even the baby was behaving. It was almost eight in the evening, so as usual, Tamera was at her desk, completing her homework and waiting on Dalton's call. She took a break from her mathematics assignment and clicked on one of the photos he'd emailed that evening. Since he'd relocated to San Pedro, they'd started exchanging selfies on a regular basis. One was of him flexing his muscles with a big smile popped up on the screen. He was bare-chested, and hamming it up for the camera. Tamera picked up the phone the moment it rang, knowing it was him.

"You like the photo?" Dalton asked.

"I especially like the one of you posing like a body-builder," she said.

"You look great in the two you sent me, but when are you going to send one that's a little more daring?" he teased. "I miss you so much. It's going to make me real happy, especially when I'm lonely."

"You're going to see me when you come home for my family get-together, so you won't be lonely then."

"Tammy," his voice softened. "I'm real sorry," he paused, "but I have to cancel my trip home this weekend. I have to work."

"You're not coming?" Tamera could not disguise the disappointment in her voice.

"I don't have a choice," he said. "My boss asked me to work, and a family function's not a good enough excuse to turn down the work."

"But you promised me you'd be here," she moaned.

"I know I did, but it's not the end of the world. There's going to be many more family gatherings in the years to come."

That evening while climbing into bed, Tamera heard the high-pitched wail of an ambulance speeding past her home. The sound reminded her of the first time her mother had been hospitalized. It was a traumatic experience, but thankfully she'd overcome the shame she initially felt when her friends found out that her mother was suffering from a mental illness. She was grateful that her mother seemed better now, but she went to bed with an uneasy feeling in her stomach, sad that Dalton would not be able to visit on the weekend.

On the day of the get-together, she woke up at six in the morning determined not to let Dalton's absence from the family get-together dampen her spirits. She was looking forward to seeing relatives she hadn't seen in ages and decided to concentrate on their pending arrival rather than on her boyfriend's cancellation. By eight, the clear skies indicated the weather was going to co-operate. And by ten the sun was at full blast; a refreshing breeze kept everyone in good spirits.

"It's a glorious Saturday," Earl said when Charlie, their first guest, arrived. Charlie shared the news that the ambulance Tamera had heard a few nights previous had gone to LaToya's house. LaToya was still missing.

"And now Cynthia's in the hospital," Charlie said. "But I'm not sure how serious it is."

When Azura's family arrived, her mother, Rachel, handed Alison a white box. "I baked a Jelly Belly Flower Cake," Rachel said.

"My mom's good enough to open her own bakery," Azura said clutching her iPad.

"You never leave that behind," Tamera laughed, pointing to her cousin's tablet.

Azura simply hugged it to her chest. "You're right about that," she snorted. "It's in-dis-pen-sa-ble!"

Tamera and Mary's aunt, Leila, and her daughter, Helena, climbed out of Leila's Volkswagen Jetta. Helena's eyes sparkled like the sun reflecting off metal. She threw back her thick curly hair, revealing her long, thin neck. The natural strands of her hair, which were as smooth, thick, and as shiny as a horse's mane, tumbled halfway down her back. Her rose-print cotton dress, tapered at the waist, fit her body like a glove. Leila's hair was as short as a soldier's, and several layers of a thick gel made it appear glossy. She always wore clothes that were a bit too big for her. Mary and Tamera had never seen her in a dress, skirt, heels, or leggings, and that day was no different. Despite the differences between mother and daughter, no one could deny that they had almost identical deep-set almond eyes.

Earl had seasoned the fish and chicken in advance. He and his brothers barbecued, and Alison helped Mary chop the vegetables for the grand salad. Tamera took pictures, which she planned to post online so that her relatives who were unable to join them could see what they'd missed. By two in the afternoon, almost everyone who had been invited was present. Two of Earl's cousins who lived in Barbados had graced the family with their presence. Jan, Azura, and Tamera limed together mostly under a tent that Renwick and Clyde had helped Earl set up behind the house. Helena hung out mostly with other relatives who she rarely spent any time with.

"You're still keeping in touch with him?" Jan asked after Azura shared several photos on her tablet of Kyle, the young man she'd befriended at the beach.

"We're email friends," she said. "There's no point in wanting more, 'cause he lives in the States."

"But didn't you say that he was planning to come here to study?" Jan said.

"Yeah," Azura said, "but I think that was more his parents' idea than his."

"You'd surely date him if you could, wouldn't you?" Tamera said.

"Maybe," she replied with a mischievous grin.

"You could marry him and get your green card to live in America," Tamera giggled.

"I'd never marry someone just to live in another country," Azura said. "Marriage isn't something to play around with. It's real serious business."

"Then why do so many people get divorced?" Jan said. "My parents still refuse to go to counselling. They refuse to give their marriage another try, no matter how much I beg them."

"I don't know what to tell you," Azura said. For a moment, the girls remained silent, empathizing with their friend's distress. Tamera patted Jan's hand, and Azura changed the subject.

"You never kept me posted regarding your father's land that Kyle's parents came to see," Azura said. "What's the lowdown on that?"

"The day after they looked at it, they phoned Pa and said that they wanted to make an offer, but they couldn't commit because an emergency came up and they had to rush back to America. And we never heard from them again."

"Neither of you understand what it's like for your parents' marriage to fall apart," Jan cut in. "That's why you both easily ignored my feelings."

"You're right," Azura said, looking directly at Jan. "Tamera and I have never experienced what you're going through, but that doesn't mean we don't care about you. And even though our parents are together, we have issues and challenges at home too."

"Mary and Renwick are still together, even though at times they fight cats and dogs," Tamera said. "Sometimes I think it would be better for them to separate rather than to continue bickering the way they do."

"You're saying that just because you don't like Renwick," Jan snorted and then ran out of the tent.

"I know for a fact that Uncle Charlie's now seeing someone else," Azura whispered. "Last weekend I overheard him mention it to my dad."

"You think she knows?" Tamera asked, wide-eyed.

"Sure she does," Azura said. "That's probably why she's in such a nasty mood."

"But she didn't say anything to me, and we talk 'bout almost everything."

"She's living in denial," Azura said, keeping her voice low.

"What are you two doing here?" Alison said as she and Rachel joined the two girls under the tent. Alison and Rachel were close friends, having grown up in the same town, and they had spent most of the day in each other's company.

"Did you all upset Jan?" Alison asked.

"Me, upset her?" Tamera touched her chest. "Never!"

"Did either of you?" Alison's eyes darted from her daughter to her niece.

"Of course not," Azura said.

"Well, she slipped out the gate with a sour face," Rachel said. "We thought one of you might have said something to hurt her feelings."

"We're not little kids anymore," Azura said. "Why would we do something like that?"

Alison shrugged. "Maybe you didn't mean any harm, but you might have said something that troubled her."

"We didn't do anything, Ma," Tamera insisted. "Jan still hasn't gotten over her parents' separation, and that's not our fault."

# 11.

TAMERA WASN'T LATE, yet she rushed out of the house, adrenaline pumping through her veins. She wanted to get to the school three-quarters of an hour before the start of her final examination. She needed to review her mathematics study notes. It was her seventh exam and Jan's ninth.

As she marched down the staircase, a van sped by, splashing water up and onto the sides of the street. She unlatched the gate, carefully stepping on the water-soaked pavement. She noticed a beaten-up poster on the light post nearest to her home, and a lump formed in her throat. The formerly lustrous poster had lost its glow, but LaToya's bold features were still quite visible. *You should be writing finals with us today,* Tamera thought sombrely. LaToya's relatives, classmates, and close friends were convinced that she was still alive. But her mother, Cynthia, had not returned to work since the night her daughter went missing.

"I've gotta focus on my stupid exam," Tamera said to herself. "I can't let anything distract me." She forced her eyes off the poster and walked at a steady pace, occasionally glancing at the mathematic formulas she had jotted down on the paper she clutched in her hand, repeating them in her head.

"What did you think?" Tamera said as she and Jan shuffled out of the exam hall, surrounded by their classmates, all of whom were comparing notes about the exam.

"It wasn't too bad," Jan replied. Her face was glowing so Tamera knew she had probably done quite well. "What about you?" Jan asked politely.

"I did my best," Tamera smiled faintly. She was instead convinced she'd messed up on more than a few of the questions, but she didn't want to spoil the rest of the day by dwelling on it too long. Jan had always been the smarter one.

*What's done is done,* she thought and she stuffed the exam questions into her pocket.

Many of Tamera and Jan's classmates were almost zombie-like as they filed out of the school. Tamera was comforted by the realization that the exam wasn't easy for a lot of her friends. So, she wasn't the only one who was worried.

"Three months of freedom for me now," Jan announced as she marched down the staircase ahead of Tamera.

Jan's father insisted that after completing her CSECs, Jan had to return to school in September and enroll in the two-year program that would prepare her for the CAPE exams and allow her to apply to a university. Tamera was of the opposing view.

"But you're going to have a better chance at life if you get a really good education," Jan had said months earlier, after Tamera had categorically stated that a university degree wasn't always essential. Jan's parents insisted that if she didn't get the required CSEC grades to advance to form six to study for CAPE, she would have to repeat form five until she got the grades necessary to get into the CAPE program. In Tamera's household, Mary had left school with only four passes, and neither Earl nor Alison had ever tried to persuade her to go back. Tamera had decided she was going to resist if her parents tried to force her to return to school in September.

Her grades had fallen considerably during her mother's last hospitalization, but after Alison was discharged, Tamera's concentration improved. And as the days passed, and her mother remained stable, she had gradually stopped worrying about her mom relapsing and her marks picked up.

But as she and Jan walked home after her final exam, she couldn't stop herself from wondering why her mom had been roaming the corridors of their house the previous night while Tamera was reviewing her formulas for the exam.

"Stop dreaming and listen to what I'm saying," Jan said, tugging on Tamera's arm.

"Sorry," Tamera nodded and turned to face her. "I was just thinking about something."

"Exams are over," Jan said. "You've got to relax."

"I waited so long for this day, and it doesn't feel as good as I thought it would," Tamera muttered.

"Take a few moments and let it sink in that school's over," Jan said.

"I'm really worried about Ma," Tamera blurted. "I think she's getting sick again."

"How come you're so worried all of a sudden? You told me she was a lot better." Jan's eyes narrowed. "Isn't she taking her medication?"

"Mary makes sure that she's taking her pills. But I'm beginning to wonder if by chance she's been tucking them under her tongue and spitting them out when Mary's not paying attention."

"If she was doing that, she'd already have had a relapse," Jan said. "Let's go down by the water so you can clear your head."

The girls swung around the bend, and made their way along the uneven ground of the dirt road leading to their special spot on the beach. Jan tapped Tamera's arm. "Have you decided what you're going to do in September yet?"

"I'm going fishing with Pa," Tamera said casually.

"Come on, Tammy," Jan said. "Let's be serious. Your father will never let you work on his boat."

"I know, but it doesn't hurt to imagine."

"Why waste time thinking about something that's never

going to happen? Maybe you're going to be better off doing CAPE while you're trying to figure out what you want to do with your life."

"You've gotta be crazy to suggest that to me."

"It's just a thought," Jan said. "You can't just stay home and do nothing, 'cause that would be a boring way to live."

"Are you the same person who promised not to bother me about going back to school?"

"I'm just trying to change your mind," Jan said. "I don't want you to make a decision you're gonna regret for the rest of your life."

When the got to the beach, the girls sat on a rock, taking in the vast expanse of blue-green ocean against the white sand. In the distance, several of their schoolmates were sprawled out on blankets, taking in the sun. An array of colours bounced off the water as others splashed and played in the gentle waves that rolled in.

"I've gotta start organizing the clutter in my room," Jan said as they watched two of their classmates wade into the water and dive under a wave.

"Your dad knows now that you're planning to go live with your mom?"

"I don't know how to tell him."

"But you have to."

"I know that it's gotta be done, but I don't want to hurt his feelings," Jan said. "I still have a week to break the news to him."

"You've gotta be out of your mind." Tamera stood up. "You can't wait till the day you're leaving to tell him."

"I'll tell him that I'm going to stay with Mom for a week, and then extend my visit."

"He's going to realize you've gone for good if you take all of your belongings."

"That's why I only plan on taking a few things."

"You'd better just tell him the truth and get it over with,"

Tamera said. She loved her Uncle Charlie and she knew how upset he would be.

"Our fathers may be brothers, but they're very different," Jan said.

"I know, but it's always better to be straight up."

"I'm going to figure it out," Jan said. "I need to sleep on it, okay?"

"I'm going to miss you after you're gone," Tamera sighed.

"I'm going to miss you too," Jan said. "But, you can come to the city and visit me whenever you like."

"I surely am going to visit you at carnival time."

"You want to know a secret?"

"What?"

"My dad started dating a woman named Angela, but it didn't last very long."

"How come you didn't tell me 'bout that?"

"It's hard to talk 'bout my dad seeing anyone but Mom. I figured if I didn't talk about it then it would just go away. I was sooo happy when they broke up."

"You know he's going to date other people, right?"

"But I won't be living with him," Jan said, "so I won't have to deal with this on a daily basis. I'd rather not know to tell you the truth."

Tamera and Jan joined their classmates who were liming closer to the water. They remained on the beach for almost two hours before heading home. As Tamera walked up the staircase to her front door, she thought of Jan's words and knew her cousin was right when she had said that it would be boring to stay at home for an indefinite period after leaving school with no plans in sight.

Dalton slipped into her thoughts as she entered the front door. He had picked up more hours at work and was now frequently unable to return to La Cresta every other weekend like he used to. Tamera cherished those times they spent together when he came back to the village. She had noticed that his calls were fewer and he didn't text her as often either. Tamera was familiar with the names of his new friends, and she often imagined what they looked like and what they talked about when he went out with them. He recently gotten his first passport and planned to spend the Independence Day weekend in Barbados with a couple of his workmates. He'd also flown to the sister island, Toledo, with his friends several times. She had wished she could join him, but of course her parents would not give their permission. She desperately wanted to make decisions independent of her parents.

"Ma," Tamera called out, hurrying into the living room, and looking everywhere for signs of her mother. There was no response, so she searched the entire house. When she realized that her mom was in the shower, she went to her bedroom and shut the door.

Dalton remained on her mind as she peeled off her red-and-white tie and her stuffy white blouse and blue skirt, her school uniform for the past five years. She wanted to burn each piece of the uniform in a large bonfire behind the house. Since that wasn't practical, she dumped her clothes in a hamper in the corner of her room. She hadn't washed any of her dirty clothes for the past two weeks because she had spent most of her time cramming for finals. She changed into a pair of fresh shorts and a T-shirt and stepped out of her bedroom, closing the door to conceal the chaos.

"How are you, Ma?" Tamera stepped into the kitchen.

"Good now, but last night the runs had me back and forth to and from the toilet."

"That's why you were walking up and down the corridor?" Tamera smiled.

"Yeah," Alison said. "I stayed up half the night because of the beef roti your sister bought me."

"I'm glad, Ma."

"That I had a diarrhea?" Alison looked questioningly at Tamera.

"I'm real glad that you're feeling better and it wasn't something worse."

"Enough about me," Alison said. "How was your math exam?"

"So-so." Tamera gestured with her hands.

"As long as you did your best, that's all that matters," her mother said. "You're ready to eat?"

"Yes, thanks," Tamera said.

Alison dished out a plateful of rice and peas and stewed beef. Tamera poured herself a glass of mauby and dashed hot pepper sauce on the edge of her plate. She sat at the kitchen table and ate in silence, thinking about the long holiday months ahead of her.

# 12.

MARY'S BABY BUMP WAS GROWING, and she and her husband were keeping their fights to a minimum. Mary had started attending church on a regular basis and Tamera wondered if that was why she and Renwick were fighting less.

Mary and Tamera were Roman Catholics, but Mary had started participating in services at an evangelical church. Tamera thought that the church members behaved as if they were the only ones who were going to Heaven, and everyone else was Hell-bound. Mary had revamped her entire wardrobe. "Women should be properly attired," she told Tamera when she'd asked her why she was all of a sudden dressing so frumpy. She had discarded every pair of pants she owned as well as her tops that exposed even a tiny bit of cleavage, and she no longer wore jewellery, except for her wedding ring. Her dresses and skirts now touched her ankles, and almost all of the other women who frequented that church adopted the same dowdy dress code.

"Why you don't come to church with me this Sunday?" Mary sat on her parents' sofa next to her younger sister.

"I don't think so," Tamera said.

"I'm getting baptized soon, and I want you to be there to support me," Mary pleaded.

"I'll let you know if I change my mind," Tamera replied,

hoping that would satisfy her sister for now.

"We're having a special service tonight. A guest preacher and a couple of singers from the States are going to be present. Come with an open mind, and if you enjoy the service then you can decide whether you want to come back on Sunday morning."

After a bit of coaxing, Tamera finally agreed to accompany her sister to the evening service. She had to admit she was curious about the American singers that would be performing. Mary pinned up her younger sister's braids in an elegant style, and Tamera slipped into a simple blue-and-white dress that Azura had given her on the day she turned sixteen.

"You look so sophisticated," Mary said as she took a few steps back and admired her handiwork. Tamera smiled wryly, but as she walked out the front door ahead of her sister she stood a bit taller. Renwick was standing next to his car in blue jeans torn at both knees and a crinkly white T-shirt.

"What time do I need to pick you up?" he said.

"Nine o'clock sharp." Mary buckled Emma into her seat.

"See you at nine, then," he said as he pulled up in front of the Gospel Worship Centre. Mary and Tamera climbed out of the car, and Renwick drove off with Emma sound asleep in the back seat.

"Why Renwick doesn't ever come to church with you?" Tamera asked.

"He just doesn't want to, and I can't force him," Mary said. "When I tried to convince him, all we did was fight. And I have now vowed to keep all arguments to a minimum."

It was the very first time Tamera had entered the Gospel Worship Centre, but there were many familiar faces; numerous fellow villagers were members of the church.

Tamera wanted to sit in the last row, but Mary shook her head and reached for Tamera's arm. "Let's get a bit closer," she said, gesturing to the front of the sanctuary. Tamera quietly followed her sister, and they settled in the middle of a pew that was mostly empty.

The service started about ten minutes after they took their seats. The choir began to belt out prayer and worship songs. Tamera didn't know any of the tunes by heart, but a big screen in front of them displayed the words and allowed her to sing along. A smartly dressed couple from Minnesota performed four songs, accompanied by the church band. A twenty-some-thing New Yorker followed the couple, and sang two more uplifting tunes.

"Do we have any first-time visitors?" the senior pastor asked.

"Stand up." Mary nudged Tamera's arm.

"No," Tamera said under her breath. But she sensed that members of the congregation seated closest to them were staring at her, so she reluctantly rose to her feet. Two women in the same pew stood up as well.

"We welcome all first-time visitors. We have a gift and light refreshments for all of you, so after the service please feel free to come to our meeting room. Just enter through the second door to the left of the sanctuary."

Tamera tried to listen attentively to the sermon, but her mind strayed every couple of minutes. Most of it was pretty boring. But she enjoyed the music and she even tried to sing along. At the end of the service, the choir flowed down the aisle in two files, singing like angels.

"We're going to the meeting room," Mary insisted.

"I don't want to," Tamera whispered.

"We're already here." Mary lowered her voice too. "Don't behave like you and Emma are twins."

"Good to see you, Tammy," Joshua's wife said as she shook Tamera's hand and then led them both to the meeting room. "Sister Mary, thank you so much for bringing her along," she added with a big smile and a nod to Mary.

As they entered the generous space, a neatly dressed man came toward them and greeted Mary. "This is my little sister, Tammy," Mary said to the man.

"I'm Pastor Williams, the youth pastor at GWC. Help yourselves to whatever you like." He pointed to a large table at the back of room overflowing with food and drinks.

"Thank you." Tamera eyed three different types of cupcakes, pondering which one to sample.

"The chocolate one's looking delicious," Mary cooed and scooped up one of the rich brown cupcakes. "It tastes really good," she said with her mouth full.

"I think I'm going to try another one," Tamera said as she helped herself to a lemon cupcake that melted in her mouth. She filled a disposable cup with pineapple juice, and Mary sipped on orange juice.

"This is a small token from us," Pastor Williams said, handing Tamera a narrow box. He offered a similar one to at least fifteen people, including the two women who were seated in the same pew as Mary and Tamera and had also identified themselves as first-time visitors.

"Let's see what you got." Mary eagerly took the box and pulled out a pen engraved with the words *Gospel Worship Centre*. "I'm going to pee," she suddenly announced and returned the pen, then rushed to the bathroom. Tamera stood in silence in the crowded room, anxiously awaiting her sister's return.

Pastor Williams came toward her. "You're going to worship with us at GWC again, I hope. I'm looking forward to seeing you at next Sunday's service."

Tamera forced a smile but didn't reply. She couldn't bring herself to meet his inquiring eyes, even though he seemed nice.

"Mary never mentioned that she had a younger sister," he said. "What are you doing over the school break?"

"Nothing special."

"You're welcome to attend our camp that will run for one week. Besides our Bible classes for teens, sports, and other interesting activities, we also need smart, youthful volunteers to help with the younger kids."

After another moment of silence, he added, "Every year we take the kids on at least one big outing, and we're planning to wrap up our camp this year with a weekend in Toledo."

"I've never been on a plane," Tamera said.

"Then this might just be your chance to get your wings," he said encouragingly.

Mary finally reappeared, looping her arm around her sister's elbow and smiling sweetly at the pastor.

"Sunday is your special day," he said to her, reaching out to pat her hand.

"I'm finally ready to take the plunge," she beamed.

"Pastor Williams is so nice. He needs a good wife," Mary said, stepping out the church door.

"I'm not interested in his life," Tamera growled.

"Tamera Williams has a really good ring to it."

"That would never happen," Tamera said. "And I don't like your church, 'cause everyone there dresses as if they're living in Amish town. And he's way too old for me anyhow."

"He's only twenty-three," Mary said. "And don't you think he's super good-looking?"

"He got an okay face, but he's a preacher, and you of all people know that I already have a boyfriend."

"Dalton?" Mary smirked. "Do you know what he's been doing since he moved to San Pedro? You only see him a couple hours every month. You need a Christian man to take care of you, someone who will never cheat on you."

"Pastors sometimes cheat on their wives too," Tamera said. "How are you so sure he wouldn't do that?"

"He's a godly man," Mary said. "His focus is helping, not hurting."

"I don't care if he's as holy as God. I have no interest in him. Dalton loves me, and we're going to get married one day."

"You're too young to know what's good for you."

"You married Renwick at eighteen, so why can't Dalton and I do the same?" Tamera's voice cracked. It went up much higher than she expected.

"I'm real sorry if I upset you," Mary said. "But you're my little sister, and I love you more than you know. I don't want you to make the same mistakes I made."

"Dalton's not a mistake," Tamera said. "Our family and his get along really well, but Ma and Pa and Renwick's parents don't get along, so our situation is not the same."

"Come on, Tammy. Because our parents and Dalton's are on good terms, it doesn't mean he's right for you," Mary said. "You've known him all your life. Maybe there's a better catch in the sea if you just open your eyes. Dad warned me about Renwick, and I didn't listen, and it's only because I'm a Christian now and I believe in the sanctity of marriage that I'm staying with him. Please don't do like me and mess up your life."

"I don't want to talk about this anymore."

"I hope you haven't slept with him," Mary said. "Have you, Tammy?"

"No, we haven't, and when we decide to do it I wouldn't tell you, 'cause it's none of your business."

"You'd better not do it, 'cause it's a sin to have sex out of marriage," Mary said. "Be careful and don't get pregnant, 'cause if you do, he's probably going to ask you to have an abortion, and that's an even bigger sin."

"If your mouth keeps going ninety miles a minute, I'm going to take the bus home!" Tamera yelled.

"I said what I had to say, and that's that," Mary said.

The sisters waited in angry silence in front of the church, avoiding each other's eyes.

"Shouldn't Renwick already be here?" Tamera eventually asked.

"He's still got a few minutes." Mary glanced at her watch. "It's only five to nine."

Renwick pulled up in front of the church at the appointed time. That evening the sisters parted, maintaining their silence

# 13.

"JAN'S MOVING IN WITH HER MOTHER," Charlie said. "She's heading to the city at the end of the week." He settled on the living room sofa, his face serious as he broke the news to Tamera's parents.

"Moving to the city will be good for her. It's also important for teenage girls to be close to their mothers," Alison said. "And the city offers a lot more opportunities than we have up here."

"I know that," Charlie nodded, his lips drawn tight. He remained silent, his head lowered. When he looked up, his eyes were glassy. "But she's my one and only child, and I'm surely going to miss her."

"Letting her go is the right thing to do," Alison said firmly.

Earl and Charlie gulped down a beer while Alison sipped from a tall glass of water. The television was on and a news announcement caught their attention. "What's that about?" Charlie stared at the television.

"Thousands of giant leatherbacks have been killed. Stay tuned for more after the commercial break," a reporter announced.

"I don't believe it." Charlie's eyes became dark and fiery.

When the news resumed, the reporter explained that during the previous evening several thousand leatherback turtle eggs and hatchlings were crushed by heavy machinery along one of the island nation's beaches. "They bulldozed the land to redirect the river to save a hotel?" Charlie pursed his lips. "This is plain madness."

"They botched the job," a conservationist said to the reporter. "They dug up the nesting beach where the leatherbacks laid their eggs."

Charlie's face remained tense and strained, and for a moment Tamera wondered if Azura, who had a special love for the gentle giants, would have a similar expression when she heard about the turtles' sad fate.

"Close to twenty thousand eggs were destroyed." The whites of the conservationist's eyes seemed to turn black as the words left his mouth.

"That is a real tragedy," Alison said as she sat up straight on her recliner, her arms tightly crossed against her chest.

"What's a tragedy?" Mary slipped through the front door carrying Emma and lowered her smiling daughter to the floor.

"Come here, Emma," Tamera gestured with her hands. Emma looked at her young aunt and smiled but she was glued to her mother's legs.

"Thousands of leatherbacks were killed after government workers bulldozed the beach to redirect the river," Charlie said.

"Everybody's so upset over some dead turtles?" Mary calmly said. "I thought someone important had been killed."

Charlie's visits to his brother's house increased tenfold after Jan relocated to the city to live with her mother. One evening as he and Tamera's parents sat in the living room watching the television show *24*, Alison looked up to the ceiling, a quizzical expression on her face.

"What's that noise?" she said. "Something up there's crawling around."

"What noise?" Charlie said.

"I didn't hear anything," Earl said, sucking in his cheeks.

*Is Ma getting sick again? Is she imagining things?* Tamera quickly dismissed those thoughts when seconds later she heard a scraping above her head, and from the look on everyone else's face they heard it too.

"How long's that been up there?" Charlie asked as the sound grew louder.

"It's the first time I'm hearing it." Earl knocked three times on the ceiling with a broom.

"What are you doing?" Mary walked in. The sound stopped for a moment before starting again.

"Seems something's living in the roof," Earl said. "And it's probably rats."

"Ugh!" Tamera twisted her mouth and nose. "That's nasty."

The sound of little feet scurrying across the roof ended as suddenly as it had started, and no one heard any further movement that evening.

"Tomorrow I'm going to ask Renwick or Clyde to climb up to the roof and inspect it," Earl said.

"You need to figure out exactly where the rodents are entering," Charlie advised.

"We'll check the eaves, and as a precaution I'm going to ask Clyde to trim the branches of the mango tree that's brushing against the house."

It rained nonstop the following day, so Earl had to wait two more days before he could investigate. After Renwick examined the roof, they discovered that the rodents had entered through a hole in the eaves. Earl arranged for his two helpers to monitor the roof that night, and Tamera delayed going to sleep that evening too.

Earl stacked four chairs and carried them from the porch to the backyard. Tamera sat alongside the three men under the moonlit night. She moved her chair a few feet away when Clyde lit a cigarette. She had almost dozed off when Earl said, "That's certainly not a rat," his eyes wide.

Tamera sat upright and fixed her eyes on the animal her father was pointing to. It was the size of a house cat but it managed to easily slip through the tiny opening in the eaves. The creature had distinct features that included large, black ears, a long tail, a pale peach-coloured face, and black whiskers. Tamera had never seen an animal like that before.

"It's surely a manicou," Renwick said. "There's no doubt about that."

"We wouldn't want to turn the roof into a grave, so we're going to seal the hole tomorrow when it come out," Earl said.

Renwick and Clyde nodded.

"Look!" Renwick said about thirty seconds later as three other manicous scurried up the wall. They slipped through the same opening. "My parents' dog could easily catch those creatures," Renwick said, standing next to Earl who hadn't taken his eyes off the roof since they spied the first manicou.

"He caught at least four of them this year alone in our parents' backyard," Clyde said. "We're going to bring that dog here to hunt them, if you don't mind."

"Not a problem," Earl said. "I haven't tasted wild meat in quite some time." Earl's mouth watered as he reminisced silently about his dad who had introduced him to this delicacy when he was a young boy.

They were going to eat the thing! Tamera's jaw just about dropped to the floor. She shuddered involuntarily as she rose and headed to bed.

The following afternoon Renwick brought his parents' Labrador retriever, Scooter, to his in-laws' home. The large dog had a shiny black coat and a wide chest; his slightly pink ears hung close to his head, and his tail was thick at the base and narrow toward the tip. Renwick let the dog loose, allowing it to roam freely behind the family's locked gate.

"Renwick!" Mary yelled. "It's time to go. It's getting late." She stood outside her husband's car holding Emma's hand, and tapping her foot impatiently.

"I'm going to drop your sister at prayer meeting," he said to Tamera. "Keep an eye on Scooter, 'cause he often gets into trouble." Renwick dashed toward the car, and as he drove off, the dog looked at Tamera with big, expressive eyes, wagging his tail furiously, and energetically licking her legs and ankles. She hadn't been in such close proximity with Scooter before and was taken aback by his friendliness. The dog followed her around the yard as if he were her shadow, occasionally jumping up to get her attention.

"You're a big dog, but you still behave like a little puppy," she giggled, ruffling the back of Scooter's ears.

"Tamera!" Her mom's voice croaked like an old woman's.

"What's wrong, Ma?" she said as she entered the house. Alison was sitting in her armchair with her eyes clenched shut, her facial muscles tightened as if she had a pulsating headache.

"Get me some painkillers from the medicine cabinet," she said.

Tamera got the painkillers and then helped her mother to bed. "Stay with me a while," Alison insisted. Tamera grabbed a chair and pulled it close to the bed. She didn't leave the bedroom until her father arrived.

"It's been a struggle to get things done today," Earl said as he unbuckled his belt and took off his work shirt.

"Why's the back gate open?" he asked, looking pointedly at Tamera.

"It can't be," she replied. "Renwick parents' dog is back there."

"There wasn't no dog there a moment ago when I shut the gate."

"Really?" Tamera jumped up and ran out of the house. She made her way to the front yard, and shouted, "Scooter, come here right now!"

"What the hell!" Renwick had just returned and was dragging Scooter by his collar down the flight of stairs.

"The sofa's a mangled mess," Renwick said. "Scooter chewed it to pieces."

Tamera went back inside and examined the unsightly gash on the three-seater sofa. Renwick hadn't exaggerated the extent of the damage.

"Mary's going to be real mad that you left the front door open," Tamera said.

"Who left the back gate open?" Renwick said. "It surely wasn't me."

"It wasn't me either," she insisted.

"I guess it doesn't matter whose fault it is, because I'm the one who's gonna have to scrape up the cash to reupholster the sofa anyhow," Renwick sighed ruefully.

Renwick picked Mary up from church at nine that evening and by ten p.m. he was ready to join his brother, Tamera, and Earl who were sitting on folding chairs in the backyard. Scooter was sprawled in front of them.

"Everything's under control," Renwick grinned as he sank into a chair. He patted the panting dog's head affectionately and said, "You have to make up for the damage you caused today."

"The manicous aren't coming here tonight," Tamera announced as she looked at her watch. "We've been here for hours, and nothing."

"Have some patience," Renwick said. "I'm willing to bet you that at least one manicou's going to appear in this yard before midnight."

At around eleven-thirty, Scooter hightailed it toward the thick bush and vanished. Minutes later, he reappeared with a furry animal between his teeth.

"Did it bite you?" Tamera was the first to observe the drips of blood on the dog's right front leg.

"Not Scooter," Renwick confidently said. "No manicou's smart enough to get the better of him, 'cause he's an A-class hunting dog."

Scooter held the animal between his teeth, and it wiggled slightly. He dropped it on the sandy ground, where it remained completely still. He hovered over it, wagging his tail, and pawing at it with his big paws.

Earl inspected the carcass, placing it on a white bucket that had been turned upside down. It was about the same size as an average house cat, and there was a bloody gash on the side of its head. The animal's yellow under-fur was hidden by longer black guard hairs, and black whiskers protruded from its pale snout. Two large black ears stuck out of the side of its head, and its tail, Tamera noticed, like that of a giant rat, didn't have any fur. It was close to two feet long.

"Wild meat's on the menu tomorrow," Renwick said in a chirpy sing-song. "Lemme see how much this baby weighs." He laid the carcass on Earl's scale. "Exactly three pounds," he proclaimed loudly.

A few moments later, he had wedged the tail on a long piece of wood and was smoking it on his barbecue.

"You're making a forest fire just to clean one manicou?" Earl chortled when at first the fire blazed higher than expected.

After all the fur had been burned off, Renwick wiped the animal's carcass with vinegar. He severed its legs and head. He removed the internal organs and its strong scent filled the backyard. He washed its dismembered parts in vinegar water, looked across at Tamera, and explained, "This is to get rid of the bacteria."

She stood within arm's reach, keenly observing every step.

At about eleven forty-five, Charlie appeared. "You guys are having a late-night party and didn't invite me," he said as Renwick seasoned the meat and then placed it in a covered bowl, ready to be cooked the next day.

"Wild meat's on the menu tomorrow," Renwick repeated his brother's earlier words as he took the bowl into the house in order to place it into the refrigerator.

Charlie looked at Tamera. "You know that a manicou's called an opossum, and sometimes possum, in North America?"

"I didn't know that," she said.

"Its also a marsupial. It's young remain in the mother's pouch until they're mature enough."

"Like a baby kangaroo?" she asked.
"You got that right."
Tamera was now almost sorry about the manicou's fate.

The following evening, they all devoured the curried wild meat, which melted on their tongues. "It tastes like beef, but it's so much leaner," Tamera said, licking her fingers one by one, all concerns for the manicou having gone by the wayside.

# 14.

FOUR WEEKS HAD PASSED since Tamera had written her final exam. She was glad that school was out, and that she didn't have to get out of bed early in the morning, but after several weeks with no specific goals or plans to keep her occupied, she was running out of new things to do and she began to feel bored. She tried to keep herself busy by helping her mother prepare the meals and clean the house, but she didn't want to spend another week doing just that. There wasn't a day that she didn't think about Jan or Dalton, and she hardly ever went to the beach anymore, because whenever she did, she felt empty inside.

So, when Alison handed Tamera a shopping list and said, "Could you please pick these things up?" Tamera jumped at the chance. She strolled to the lone shop in the tiny fishing village, owned by Joshua and his wife, and located on the lower floor of their two-storey home. The Joshuas sold a variety of dried goods, including basic staples like rice and flour, but they barely stocked any fruits or vegetables, since most of the villagers planted their own crops and traded directly with their neighbours. The closest major supermarket was more than an hour away on foot, and that was probably the main reason why the Joshuas did such brisk business.

"Hi there," a male voice called out in greeting as Tamera walked by Samuel's house. She wasn't sure if the man was talking to her, but her eyes looked toward the young man who seemed about ten years older than her. He was of medium build, had short, curly hair, and wore a big, pleasing grin. He was staring genially at Tamera from behind Samuel's gate.

"You live across there?" He spoke with a North American accent, pointing to her home.

"Yeah," she replied.

"I noticed when you stepped outside," he said. "I'm Matthias, and I'm here visiting my uncle. I live in San Pedro." He paused for a moment. "What's your name?"

"Tamera."

"Matthias!" a woman yelled from inside the house. "Come, we're ready for you right now."

"See you around," he said. "I gotta go in." He waved then spun around. She was sure she'd seen him somewhere before, but couldn't quite figure out where.

She continued on her way to Joshua's shop, rattling her brain about where she might have met that guy before. As she entered the store, she noticed the words *Teenagers, you are invited to Gospel Church Camp* stamped in big letters on a bright green flyer that was taped to the wall right next to the door.

"Have you registered yet?" Mrs. Joshua stood behind the red counter that separated her from her customers.

"No," Tamera said.

"Well, you'd better hurry up and do it soon," she said gruffly.

Tamera smiled and ignored the comment. She read out the goods on her list, and Mrs. Joshua pulled them off the shelves. "Anything else?" Mrs. Joshua said.

"No, that's it," Tamera said, then added her thanks.

Mrs. Joshua packed Tamera's purchases in a shopping bag and placed a copy of the green flyer on top. Tamera waited until she left the store before pulling the flyer from the top of the bag. She folded it into a tiny square, and tucked it into her purse. She wasn't sure why she'd kept it instead of dumping it in the garbage.

On her way back, she slowed down as she came to Samuel's house, her eyes darting around the yard, hoping to catch another glimpse of Matthias, but she didn't see anyone. Her heart sank. She wanted so much to ask him if he remembered meeting her before. When she got to her porch, it clicked. He was the lanky guy she and her friends had admired at the wire-bending exhibition. She was sitting on the porch, hoping to see him come out of the house when her cell phone rang.

"What's up?" It was Jan.

Tamera was happy to hear her voice "I met the same good-looking guy who was at the wire-bending exhibition," she replied. "You remember him?"

"Of course," Jan said.

"Well, he told me that his name is Matthias, and he lives in San Pedro," Tamera said. "He's got a cute American accent."

"He does?" Jan said.

"He looks just as hot as he did that day."

"You've never described any guy as hot before, except for Dalton," Jan snickered. They talked and giggled for a while before Tamera had to go inside and put away the shopping.

After the shopping had been dealt with, Tamera joined her parents in their sprawling yard behind the house, where they were harvesting hot peppers. For a while, her thoughts remained on Matthias. Jan was right. It was the first time she'd felt any interest in anyone other than Dalton, and it was weird. She couldn't explain it, even to herself. She helped her parents pile the peppers in a large oval basket and Tamera noticed that Alison's face glowed. Tamera hadn't ever seen her mother look so healthy before. And happy. She was enjoying the afternoon it seemed. Tamera knew that Alison saw her psychiatrist regularly, and that he'd recently adjusted her medication. Maybe it was helping and Tamera felt encouraged to see that Alison had also resumed more of the activities she used to enjoy before the illness took control of her life, like gardening and volunteering at the local elementary school. By the time Tamera and her parents had finished working in the garden, Matthias had slipped out of her mind.

That afternoon, she helped her sister season the chicken for a pelau dish she was preparing for a church function. Mary had picked up most of her cooking tips from their mother, and Tamera wanted to be as good a cook as they were. Since she'd finished her exams, her cooking skills had improved dramatically, and she was proud of that. She was almost an expert at making numerous dishes, but she especially enjoyed preparing macaroni pie, a dish with pasta, eggs, milk, and lots of melted cheese. The pelau they were preparing was also a favourite: a one pot dish of pigeon peas and chicken cooked with coconut milk and herbs. But she hadn't wanted to develop her culinary skills solely for the bragging rights; she wanted to be able to prepare the most wonderful meals for Dalton.

She knew that if her dream to marry him came true, she wouldn't be able to depend on him to cook. When he had relocated to San Pedro to work, he barely knew how to boil water and in recent months he had confessed that his culinary skills were pretty much non-existent.

The following morning, it rained for almost an hour, but by noon the sun was out. Tamera slipped out the backdoor. With her head hung low, she observed a row of industrious black ants chipping leaves and carrying them in an organized line. She was tempted to disturb the unbroken line of working ants, but Mary interrupted her. "Why are you looking as if it's the end of the world?" She was wearing a long green-and-white cotton dress that flapped around her ankles. "Stop it," she said to her fidgeting daughter, who was slung over one hip, and had almost slipped out of her arms.

"You made up your mind yet?" Mary asked as she shifted the child to her other hip. Tamera looked at her sister blankly. She wasn't sure what Mary was talking about and she wasn't in the mood to dance around some topic.

"Are we on the same planet?" Mary stepped closer, and a strong gust of wind took hold of her dress, swinging the full skirt around her legs. She gathered the skirt with both hands, pulling it to her side. "Put on a pretty dress and let's go to church," she ordered.

"I don't think so."

"You'd rather sit behind the house feeling sorry for yourself?" Tamera didn't answer, and didn't even look up.

"Your choice," Mary said as she began to walk away. Suddenly she stopped and, looking back at her sister, she added, "The church camp's starting in a week. I'm not going to waste time reminding you again."

"Come and answer your phone!" Alison shouted, her head hanging out of the window. Tamera rushed inside, but by the time she got there, her phone had stopped ringing.

It was Jan. Tamera called her back. "I just missed your call," she said, almost breathless.

"Where were you?" Jan asked. "I've been trying to reach you for quite some time."

"I left my phone on the bed and went outside."

"I have a favour to ask," Jan said. "It's my dad's birthday on Saturday. Do you mind coming over and helping me to make a nice meal for him?"

"Not at all."

"Cool," Jan said. "You're still up for the trip to the cave, even though we're no longer going to the one where you have to climb down a rope?"

"You bet," Tamera said. "I've been counting down the days for the past couple of weeks. I wish we could go there right now."

"Azura's still not coming, so it's going to be just you, me, and Dad."

"It's hard to believe that Azura's changed so much," Tamera said. "She's surely lost her sense of adventure." She shook her head as she shut the phone, but she was pleased to have something exciting and fun to look forward to.

After the call, she went to her bedroom and pulled the green church flyer from her wallet. She and unfolded it and laid it down on the table in her room. She stared at it for several minutes, wondering if she should surprise her sister and register for the camp. *Is it worth torturing myself for a whole week just to be able to have one weekend of fun in Toledo?*

She weighed the pros and cons in her head. "It's not worth it," she said to herself. She crumpled the leaflet and tossed it into the garbage.

That evening, Dalton phoned Tamera earlier than he usually did. "I cut off all of my hair as a dare," he said.

"You must look weird with a bald head," Tamara laughed.

"Let's log on to Skype," he suggested. And when they did, his smile filled the screen. "I miss you so much. You have no clue how much I love you."

"Of course I do," she said. "I love you a whole lot too."

"I wish I could pull you through the computer screen and keep you in San Pedro with me all week," he said.

"Me too," she said. "But my parents would never allow it."

"I know," he said.

"Are you ever going to send me that special photo I've been waiting for?" He made a funny face. "Please make me happy tonight," he pleaded, his palms pressed together as though he were praying. "Pleeeeeease," he repeated.

"I'm gonna think about it," Tamera replied.

After logging off Skype, Tamera decided she would finally give him what he wanted. She pulled off her top and shorts and positioned her camera on its tripod. In her skimpy underwear, she snapped a few pictures of herself in suggestive poses. She hoped Dalton would like them. She was about to upload them to her computer when the power went.

Earl sucked his teeth. "What bad timing!" he yelled from the living room. "We're on the brink of beating Australia for once, and the electricity has gone."

Tamera slipped into the clothes she'd removed minutes earlier and headed into the living room. Several minutes later, the power returned. Her dad switched on the television, but the cricket match had already ended.

"I can't believe I missed this," Earl said, but he was happy that the West Indies had won. "This doesn't happen too often anymore," he said beaming and taking in the jubilant faces on the television screen.

Mary rushed in the house clutching her daughter by the hand. "Tammy," she said. "You mind watching Emma for about an hour? I've got something important to take care of."

"Not a problem." Tamera led her niece to her room and plopped her onto the bed. She grabbed a bunch of picture books she kept on the shelf for Emma, and patiently read to her from each of them, cooing over the pictures and coaxing her to repeat some of the words.

"Tired," Emma yawned and blinked sleepily.

"I hear you," Tamera said and put the books back on the shelf. Emma cruised around the bedroom, inspecting all of her aunt's belongings and giggling happily when Tamera pretended to chase her.

When Mary returned to pick up Emma and take her home, Tamera was ready to email the photos to Dalton, but she couldn't find her camera anywhere. She searched the entire bedroom without success and then phoned her sister.

"Did Emma bring my camera over there by chance?"

"Lemme check." Mary put Tamera on hold. "Yeah, you're in luck. She put it in her bag. My daughter's a kleptomaniac," Mary laughed.

"I'm going to pop over right now and get it," Tamera said.

"It's kinda late, Tammy," Mary said. "We're already in bed. I'll bring it over tomorrow."

The following morning, Mary burst through Tamera's bedroom door with stone-cold eyes. "What you're doing is totally inappropriate," she fumed, keeping her voice low. Tamera sat on her bed and looked up at her sister with a scowl on her face. "What kind of self-respecting girl takes the kind of photos you have in here, eh?" Mary threw Tamera's bright red camera at her. It bounced twice on the bed. "What if someone else found it and put those disgusting photos on the net? You're real lucky I did you a favour and deleted all of them. I hope you smarten up and don't take such filthy pictures like that again."

Tamera lowered her eyes, heavy with shame. Mary had seen the photos meant for Dalton's eyes only. "I-I-I was just playing around," she said. "I-I-I was going to delete them last night, but I couldn't find the camera."

"You'd better start going to church," Mary snarled, slamming the door behind her when she left.

"I just arrived at my dad's house," Jan said to Tamera over the phone later that day.

"How come you got here so late?" Tamera said.

"It's Dad's fault," Jan replied. "He didn't get to my place till after seven."

"Oh, I see."

"What time are you coming here tomorrow to help me cook?" Jan asked.

"What time do you want me come?"

"Around ten would be perfect."

"I've gotta go, 'cause Dalton's on the other line," Tamera said.

"What happened to the photos?" Dalton said, barely waiting for Tamera to greet him. "I waited all night for them," he whined

"I was going to send them, but then the power went."

"Didn't the power come back?"

She remained silent.

"Tammy?" he said. "You're there?"

"Yeah," she said. "I'm here."

"Something's wrong?"

"Look," she paused. "I thought about it and decided that it probably wasn't such a good idea after all."

"Why?" he said.

"I really don't feel comfortable about sending you those kinds of pictures," she finally admitted.

"I'm not going to share them with nobody," he said. "You don't trust that it's going to be for my eyes only?"

"You're not listening to me," she said. "I just told you that I'm not comfortable about doing that, and I don't want you to ask me again."

"Anyway, if you don't trust me, that's fine," he said, his voice firm with undisguised anger.

"You don't understand," Tamera sighed. No way was she going to tell him that Mary had found the few she had taken and deleted them.

"Sure right, I don't," he said. "It's not a good feeling not to be trusted."

"What time are you going to get home tomorrow?" she asked, hoping to change the topic.

"I can't make it," he said. "One of my workmates is in the hospital, and I have to cover for him."

"Whatever," she said, hanging up, and angry now too.

Tamera didn't sleep soundly that night. She was humiliated that Mary had come down so hard on her after seeing the photos. She was also frustrated that Dalton's second consecutive trip to La Cresta had been aborted, but she was thankful that the power had gone out the previous afternoon, preventing her from emailing the photos to him. She woke up at about five o'clock the following morning and tossed and turned for an hour before giving up on more sleep.

*Does Dalton really have to work this weekend, or is he lying?*

She took a quick early-morning shower then checked her social media accounts before playing her favourite typing game.

She didn't stop until she heard heavy footsteps accompanied by loud voices. She left her room to investigate the cause of the commotion, and as she got to the living room, Renwick was on his way out the front door. Her father, it seemed, was not going to work.

"Pa, you're okay?" Tamera asked.

"Yeah, yeah, everything under control." Earl's eyebrows were scrunched and his lips drooped a bit. Tamera returned to her room, curious. *Why isn't he in bed?* Earl hadn't gone fishing the previous night because he had some pain on his side.

Tamera settled on her stiff mattress. Her thoughts drifted back to the conversation with Dalton the previous evening. *How am I going to be able help Jan cook a decent meal for her dad when I feel so crappy?*

About half an hour later, she joined her parents in the kitchen. Earl was speaking to someone on his cellphone. "He didn't even have the respect to give me proper notice. Two days is all I got."

"He can be replaced," Alison said.

Earl placed his phone on the table, dragged a chair over and sat, dropping his head into his cupped hands. "You're one hundred percent right 'bout that," he grunted, then scooped up a spoonful of porridge. "It's just the disrespect I don't like."

"That's how the younger generation behaves nowadays," Alison said. "They just not brought up like in the old days."

Earl was upset because Renwick had resigned as one of his helpers without giving him proper notice. He had secured a better-paying job at a newly opened beer factory in a neighbouring community. "Mary must have known beforehand," Earl said, and his eyebrows seemed to slip closer together. "My own daughter's been holding a secret for that waste of a man. I shouldn't have allowed them to build on my land."

"Despite everything, we can't forget that Mary's been good to us," Alison said. "I guess she owes allegiance to Renwick, because whether we like it or not, he's her husband."

"Husband?" Earl scoffed. "And all of these years it's my money that's been keeping a roof over their heads?"

The only noise in the room was Earl's slurping as he spooned porridge into his mouth. He abandoned the empty bowl on the table. "Last week Joshua told me that his wife's nephew was looking for work. I'm going over there right now to ask him if the boy wants to work on the boat."

Tamera watched as her father stormed out of the house, hopped into his car, and drove out of the yard. "Why's Pa taking the van if he's only going to Mr. Joshua's house?" she said.

"Only your dad can answer that one," Alison calmly said, her lips pressed together.

Tamera's primary focus at that moment was what her dad would say to Mary later that day. "I'm going to Uncle Charlie's place," she said, anxious to be out of the house in case things turned ugly.

# 15.

TAMERA MARCHED UP CHARLIE'S STAIRCASE admiring a wreath that was hanging on the wall. It was made up of pretty red, yellow, purple, and white flowers complemented by verdant green leaves. A tiny hummingbird, kiskadee, scarlet ibis, macaw, heron, and even a little pelican, made of paper maché, were tucked in among the flowers and leaves. Tamera couldn't take her eyes off it even as she knocked on the front door.

"You're here!" Jan said as she opened the door.

"That's really pretty," Tamera said, pointing to the wreath.

"Yeah, it is. Dad's students gave it to him for his birthday," Jan said. "How come you're here so early?"

"Girl," Tamera paused. "I had to leave home before Dad got back."

"Why?" Jan asked. "What's up?"

"Renwick's no longer working for Pa."

"Don't tell me Uncle Earl fired him!"

"No," Tamera replied. "He resigned 'cause he found a bet-ter-paying job."

Jan's left eyebrow shot up. "Let's sit in the porch so you can give me the whole scoop." She grabbed a chair, and waved for Tamera to sit in the chair facing her. Tamera filled in her cousin on the details of Renwick's sudden resignation. "Well, well." Jan shook her head. "Uncle Earl must be as mad as hell."

Tamera nodded and Jan suddenly changed the topic. "You realize exam results are coming out soon."

"Why did you have to mention that?" Tamera groaned.

Jan chuckled gleefully. "It's going to happen whether you like it or not, so there's no point ignoring it."

Charlie strolled onto the porch. "My favourite niece is here." He pulled up a chair next to them and engaged them in some more small talk as they enjoyed the fresh air and sunlight.

"You're ready to start cooking?" Tamera asked about an hour later.

"Sure, why not?" Jan said.

"Dad, it's time to eat." Jan stood in front of the dining table decorated with a white tablecloth and a small vase of red and white hibiscus.

"You girls have made my day," Charlie grinned, his eyes running from one end of the table to the other. Abundant platters of rice and peas, baked chicken, callaloo, fried plantains, green salad, and stewed red beans made his mouth water.

"My niece and daughter are good enough to open a top class restaurant," he said as he sat down, ready to relish his dinner.

"Tammy deserves the credit, 'cause she's the real cook." Jan said.

Charlie heaped his plate with food and demolished it. "Seconds are in order," he grunted and filled his plate again. Jan and Tamera giggled as he wolfed down his food, delighted that they had made him happy.

After their meal, Jan placed a tub of ice cream and a birthday cake that Azura's mother had baked on the table, and they devoured that as well. And after dessert, the girls whiled away the afternoon playing Charlie's favourite board game, Scrabble, with him.

"It's time that we take in a movie," Charlie said after winning three quarters of the Scrabble games. He chose *Maleficent* from a box of DVDs.

When it ended, Jan selected another DVD. "Let's watch something else."

Tamera put her feet up, ready to take in *12 Years a Slave*, but suddenly she changed her mind. "You know what? We ought to watch the news to see what's happening in the world today." Charlie agreed and switched to the BBC World News, already in progress.

"Do we have to watch this?" Jan groaned when the sombre image of soldiers carrying coffins off a military plane appeared on the screen. "Call me when the news is done." She got up and left the room, somewhat disgruntled.

"It's important to know what's going on in the world, even if it's upsetting." Charlie looked at Jan disapprovingly as she slipped out onto the porch, but she didn't appear to hear him, and she quietly closed the door behind her.

"You and I are going to catch the local news." After the BBC news ended, Charlie switched the channel to a local news station. Tamera remained on the sofa, even though she wanted to join Jan on the porch.

"Officials are preparing clean-up operations after three thousand barrels of oil slipped into the Carson River last evening," the news anchor said. "At least twenty people in the area have received medical treatment for nausea and eye irritations."

"What carelessness!" Charlie hunched forward, his eyes fixed on the aerial view of a long stretch of black oil on the shores of the river. "I hope those people get compensated for their suffering. Liability has to fall somewhere between Petro Oil Company and the government."

Tamera stared at the television screen, her brow furrowed. *Thank God this is not happening in our village.*

Charlie grabbed his phone and headed out to the porch. Jan came inside. "Do you mind if I switch channels?" she said.

"Not at all," Tamera replied.

"Dad's looking angry enough to butt somebody if they stare at him too hard."

"He's upset because there's an oil spill in Carson Village."

"That's why I hate watching the news," Jan said. "They never talk about anything good."

The following day, Jan and Tamera made their way along Jonko Trail, their destination the beach. "It's really good to be here." Tamera spread a red-and-green blanket on the snow-coloured sand. "I've missed coming here with you."

"I know, "Jan said. "It's wonderful to be in my favourite place in the world and not have to worry about anything. Dad's so wrapped up about the Carson oil spill. I'm sick of his bitching. Is Uncle Earl obsessed about the oil spill too?"

"You bet," Tamera said. "Just like Uncle Charlie, he talks about it more than anything else."

They were the only people close to the shore until a group of picnickers set up blankets about fifteen feet from them. "They're from Mary's church, and that guy with the khaki shorts is Pastor Williams," Tamera whispered.

"That's him?" Jan's eyes opened wide.

"Yeah," Tamera nodded.

"I'm sure I've seen him before," Jan said. "Dalton's much taller and way better-looking though."

"Mary thinks Dalton's cheating 'cause he doesn't come home that often anymore," Tamera said, her expression glum.

"Don't let Mary put those negative thoughts into your head," Jan warned.

Jan and Tamera observed the female members of the church dressed in oversized T-shirts wearing long loose pants or leggings pulled over regular swimsuits.

"It's weird that all of them are going in the water with so much clothing on." Jan shook her head.

"I know," Tamera said. "I almost feel as if my sister's joined a cult."

Tamera touched Jan's arm. "Let's move from here," she said. "I don't want to be so close to them." The girls gathered their belongings, widening the gap between themselves and the church members.

As the sun dropped in the sky, brilliant colours streamed from the undersides of a passing cloud to the ocean floor, the waves shimmering as they rolled into shore. Tamera and Jan dipped their feet in the warm water as they started their walk home. Suddenly it began to pour, but the cousins didn't scamper off the beach like the churchgoers. They walked at a moderate pace, and by the time they arrived home the sun had returned full blast, but they were totally wet.

# 16.

"RESULTS OF THE CSECS going to be out tomorrow morning." Jan ate up her words on the phone.

"Sorry, but I've gotta go, 'cause Dalton's on the other line," Tamera said and quickly jumped back to the previous call.

"What's up?" Dalton asked.

"Thanks for saving me."

"Saving you?"

"Yeah, you saved me."

"Well, thanks for giving me credit, but I don't have a clue what I save you from."

"Jan was on the other line talking 'bout our exam results, and you know how I feel 'bout that topic."

"You're going to be fine," he laughed. "I bet you're going to be smiling all the way to school to collect your results slip after you check your grades online."

"You're still coming home this weekend?"

"Sorry." He paused. "I'm afraid I have to work on Saturday again, but it's not all bad, 'cause I'm going to make a quick trip down there on Sunday morning. The thing is, though, there's not going to be a lot of time, since I have to head back to San Pedro by early evening. I can't afford to miss work on Monday morning."

"It's better than nothing," Tamera said, grinning with happiness.

Tamera sat back in the chair in front of her computer, and for a few moments her fingers were suddenly numb. She inhaled a long, deep breath before logging on to the Caribbean Examinations Council's website. She stared at her wobbly fingers. *This is not a matter of life and death,* she told herself.

She closed her eyes, trying to calm herself. About thirty seconds later, she typed in her ten-digit registration number, last name, and date of birth. Wide-eyed and open-mouthed, she stared at her results: two ones and four twos.

"Ma!" she yelled, dashing out of the chair and bursting into the living room. "I got six passes!"

"I knew you'd do it," Alison hugged her daughter and they both smiled widely. Just then Tamera's phone rang.

She ran to her room and picked it up. "Hello," she said, pressing the phone against her ear. ,

"I passed all nine subjects and got seven ones!" Jan exclaimed.

"I got six passes," Tamera crowed. "I only failed mathematics."

"You're going to register for CAPE then?" Jan asked.

Tamera did not reply. "Tammy, are you going to register or not?"

Again, she didn't respond.

"Don't tell me you're going to be as stubborn as an ox and not register," Jan sighed.

When Dalton arrived on Sunday morning, he had a big smile on his face. "How you doing?" He took a few steps back, admiring Tamera from head to toe, sweat pouring down his temples.

"I'm good," she said and offered him a tissue.

"You look great," he said as he mopped up the perspiration dripping down his face. "And congrats. I'm so proud of you."

"Thank you," she said.

"I'm real tired after working such long hours," he said, grabbing a chair and sitting on the porch. "I can hardly wait for the Independence weekend, when me and the boys are going back to Barbados. I'm planning to have a real good weekend then."

Tamera dragged another chair and set it down next to him. He pulled his cell phone from his pocket and checked the time. "I can only stick around for about twenty minutes," he said as she sat down next to him. He swung his arm over her shoulders and added, "I'm leaving this extra newspaper here," he said. "I've gone through and thought maybe your dad would like to read it." The folded newspapers concealed more than half of the sunburst pattern on the circular table in front of them.

Just then Tamera's dad appeared the front door and eyed them both. "Good afternoon," Dalton said warmly.

"We don't see much of you these days," Earl said. "Everything's all right?"

"As you know, I don't have set work hours," Dalton explained. "And I often have to work on Saturdays, so that's why I can't travel home as much as I'd like."

Earl walked toward Tamera and Dalton and stood next to them.

"That's a horrible thing, eh?" Earl's eyes fell on the newspapers on the table. He picked it up and held it upright so that Tamera and Dalton could see the headline: *Oil Spill Killing River Marine Life.*

"Yes, I've read it," Dalton nodded. "My workmate's sisters almost died of an asthma attack due to the pollution in the Carson River," he added.

"Petro Oil Company claims to have contained the oil, but I'm not so sure we can trust what they're telling the public," Earl said. "Almost everybody's so corrupt."

"I know," Dalton said. "But I hope for the sake of the environment that the powers that be do a good job and clean up the area."

"This headline's not promising at all," Earl said, shaking his head.

Tamera fidgeted on the chair, wishing her father would retreat to his bedroom. He eventually did, but a few minutes later, Dalton stood up. "Sorry, I've gotta hit the road before it gets too late."

"You're going to take another month before you come home again?" Tamera asked plaintively.

"I don't know," he shrugged. "We've gotta wait to see my schedule."

In stunned silence, Tamera's eyes followed him as he skipped down the staircase, climbed into his car, and drove off.

Jan and Tamera rarely had any disagreements, but Jan's insistence that Tamera should return to secondary school for another two years to study for CAPE upset Tamera a lot. "You're becoming a nag," Tamera said. She and Jan walked out of the school compound after collecting the official printout of their CSEC results. "I'm going to try to find a job. I don't want to have to study for another exam ever again in my entire life."

"It's going to be really hard to find a good position without getting at least grade three in math," Jan said. "And you're not eighteen. You're not even seventeen yet."

Tamera knew Jan was right. Most ads for menial clerical positions in both government and private organizations usually required candidates to have acquired at least a bare pass in mathematics, in addition to four other subjects, and being only sixteen complicated her situation.

"At least you're gonna have to redo math," Jan insisted. "There's no way to get around that."

"I've gotta think about my next steps," Tamera replied. "But in the meantime please back off."

"Okay, okay." Jan raised both hands, palms outward. "I promise that I'm gonna give you all the space you want."

Two days later, Jan was almost breathless when she phoned Tamera. "I got accepted into Cardinal High School to study for

CAPE, and since Mom's job is sending her to St. Vincent on short notice, I'm going to come stay with Dad for an entire week."

Tamera was grateful that Jan was true to her word and was no longer pressuring her to return to school. She definitely needed time to decide what she was going to do next. But despite her surprisingly good examination results, she wasn't any closer to knowing what she wanted to do with the rest of her life.

# 17.

"I'VE NEVER SEEN YOU IN THAT top before." Tamera admired Jan's frilly pink-and-white blouse. The girls settled in the back seat of Charlie's vehicle.

"This is one of the gifts I got from Mom for passing my exams." Jan brushed the unusual top with open palms. "These new jeans and sneakers are from her too."

"Cool," Tamera said.

"What do you want your dad to get you for being such a good student?" Charlie adjusted his rearview mirror.

"My own car," Jan giggled. "And make sure it's a brand new Mercedes-Benz."

"Wow. Your taste is more expensive than my pocket," he grinned. "I guess the only thing that's gonna save me today is that you're still under the legal driving age."

"But only by a few months," Tamera teased.

"Maybe Tamera's dad can finance your Benz after he finds a buyer for his land." Charlie peeked at his watch. "If we don't get going, the other hikers we're meeting there might head up the trail without us.

"It's a really hot morning, but it's a beautiful day," he said and started the car.

"Is it okay if I wind down the window?" Tamera asked.

"No need to," Charlie said. "I'm going to switch on the AC right now."

Tamera couldn't recall ever feeling more content. This morning she was on her way to a cave in the north of the island with her uncle and cousin, and she was not going to allow herself to think about Dalton for one minute. She was determined to enjoy the outing and all it had to offer. They'd been on the road for fifteen minutes when ominously dark clouds crossed the sky. "It's not going to be fun to trek up the incline if it's wet," Charlie said as raindrops began to pelt the windshield. "Maybe it's just a passing cloud," he added.

Charlie was right and just a few minutes later, the rain stopped and the sunshine returned. They eventually arrived at a picturesque village where a rose pink nineteenth-century house with louvered shutters and myriad patterns of ornamental wood framing its large porch caught their attention. "I can just imagine what life was like here back in the day," Uncle Charlie said.

They passed a few more of these elaborate homes and Charlie had to slow down significantly to manoeuvre around the corners. The girls were too excited to complain about the bumpy road, even as the car dipped into giant potholes.

They finally reached their destination at the bottom of a big hill just outside of the village they just travelled through. "Everybody's meeting us right here," Charlie said and parked alongside a gravel pathway.

"I need to stretch my legs." Tamera climbed out of the car ahead of her uncle and cousin. Seconds later, two SUVs pulled up behind Charlie's car. Three adult men, a teenage boy, and four adult women emerged from the vehicles.

A tall, slim man introduced himself as Frank. "I'll take the lead," he said purposefully. Everyone dutifully fell in behind him. They secured their supplies and ensured their flashlights were working. Then they started the trek up the hill.

The terrain was rough. The only way to get to the top was on foot. Charlie was directly behind Frank. "Stay close by," he said to his niece and daughter. The girls gazed at the thick fog covering the hillside as they started their climb. "The mist up at the top reminds me of my visit to England," Charlie said.

One of the women suddenly got cold feet. "I don't know if I can go all the way up there."

The man next to her rolled his eyes. "If you're not going up, then you're going to have to stay in the car by yourself."

"Azura would have freaked out like her if she'd come along," Jan whispered to her cousin.

"You're sure right 'bout that," Tamera smiled.

"Anyone's going to stay with me?" The woman's voice shook a little. When no one volunteered, she said, "Okay, I'm going to try."

Climbing was a challenge. The murky track was almost as slippery as ice. Jan and Tamera slid backward a few times. They held on to parts of trees, roots, trunks, and branches to steady themselves, keeping their place directly behind Charlie. They were ahead of the woman who'd initially hesitated to climb the hill, and since several of the hikers separated her from them, the girls were unable to see her. Her partner's tone had softened and he encouraged her with each step. Tamera exhaled when she finally arrived at the top. It had taken her almost an hour. She was sure the others arriving behind her must have also puffed out a big burst of air. She waved in all directions, trying to chase away mosquitoes, but there were so many that her flailing arms didn't help much. At the peak of the hill, the hikers walked for another ten minutes to reach the cave they were aiming for.

"Look over there," Charlie said and pointed to the mouth of a cave that appeared at the base of a huge rockface. The entrance was about thirty feet high and slightly wider than that.

"The cave's made up of several chambers deep inside the mountain," Frank explained. The hikers shone flashlights, carefully making their way inside. Tamera was thankful there weren't any mosquitoes in the first chamber they entered. She tensed when a high-pitched clicking sound greeted them. "They're oilbirds," Frank said calmly. Tamera couldn't make out the exact colour of the noisy birds perched on the walls due to the poor lighting, but Frank explained that they were for the most part a dull reddish-brown with white spots. "The Amerindians in South America use the oil from these birds to provide fuel for their lamps," Frank continued. "These are the only nocturnal fruit-eating birds in the world. They navigate by echolocation in the same way as bats, and they have the unique ability to hover and twist in flight in order to get to the tighter areas of a cave."

The group paused to take in the sounds of the birds longer than Tamera would have liked. She exhaled when Frank gave the go-ahead for them to move on. She peered straight ahead and into total blackness. "Any bats in there?" she asked as she scrunched down, and entered the second chamber.

"If you go far enough inside, you might see a few of them," Charlie said.

"How come it's raining in here?" the teenage boy asked the woman who'd initially hesitated to climb up the hill.

"It's God's work," she said.

Tamera shone her flashlight in front of her and tried to identify the source of the constant flowing water. "The stalactites are the source," Frank said when she asked.

"What are stalactites?" the teenage boy said.

"They're calcium carbonate deposits shaped like icicles hanging from the roof of the cave, which are formed by the dripping of percolating calcareous water." Frank shone his flashlight directly onto the icicle-shaped deposits decorating roof of the cave and the walls around them.

"I can see them," the boy said, decidedly impressed.

"It's so much more beautiful now than when we were here several years back," Charlie said.

"Yes," Frank replied. "It's great to see so much activity. The formations seem to have built up considerably."

"You're right," Charlie added. "They've definitely elongated a little more than during our previous visit."

Frank directed his flashlight onto a cylindrical mass of calcium projecting upward from the limestone cave floor. "Those are called stalagmites, and they are also formed by the continuous dripping water," he told the group.

They explored the ceiling and walls of the second chamber for quite some time before continuing. Even though Tamera was a bit uneasy at first, she was able to relax when the plethora of bats hanging from the low roof in the third chamber remained where they were without budging.

"It's time to head back," Frank eventually said. When they arrived in the gleaming sunlight, their eyes took a while to readjust.

# 18.

AS THE HIKERS TREKKED DOWN the hillside, their armpits felt soggy, and sweat poured down their faces and chests as if they'd been sprayed with a water gun. When they were almost at the halfway mark, the sun suddenly disappeared. "I hope it says like this," Jan said. But minutes later, the sun came out and it was even hotter than before.

When they finally got back to the cars, Jan said, "I can't believe we're here already."

"It feels as if we got back here in half the time it took to get up there," Tamera exhaled, looking uphill.

"I don't know why time always seems longer when you're going somewhere rather than when you're returning," Jan said.

"I sometimes wonder about that too," Tamera nodded.

As they headed to their respective vehicles, they all waved goodbye to each other. Charlie unlocked his car and Jan climbed into the backseat. Tamera made herself comfortable in the front with Charlie.

"I need a bath," Jan said and daubed her face with a tissue. Charlie started the ignition and soon they were on the highway. "Tammy, you want to head to the beach when we get back?" Jan asked.

"Not today," she said. "I'm going to take a shower at home and then relax in my room."

"You're gonna stay in your room all afternoon?"

"I need more than just a few hours' rest. Last night I didn't fall asleep until after two, and I'm beginning to feel it. I'm real tired"

"Why did you stay up so late?"

"I just couldn't fall asleep, so I got out of bed and surfed the net."

"I guess you were playing that typing game you're hooked on again."

"I'm not hooked," Tamera said. "It's a good game. It helps me to increase my typing speed, and I'm proud to say I'm a mega-racer now."

"Congrats," Jan said. "I could never average eighty words a minute like you can."

"If you practice, you could surely do it," Tamera said. She knew Jan could do anything she wanted once she put her mind to it.

"I have no intention of spending endless hours on my computer when I could be doing outdoorsy stuff," Jan announced.

"I hope you're not upset that I don't want to go to the beach," Tamera said.

"Not really. I just thought it would be a good idea seeing as I'm going back to Port City tomorrow morning, and we're not going to have no time to lime down by the beach together until my next visit."

"When are you coming back?"

"I don't know yet."

"I hope you're gonna come back for at least a weekend before school starts, 'cause when it does you're going to be super busy with assignments and all till the Christmas break."

"Independence weekend would be an ideal time to return," Charlie said. "We could take a nice drive to see the humming-birds in action and also visit a water park."

"I'd love to, Dad, but I already made plans. Me and Mom are going to the Independence Day parade."

"Oh well," he said. "We're going to have to schedule our next trip another time."

"Tammy," Jan said, "why don't you come to the city and take in the parade with me and Mom?"

"That sounds good," Tamera said. "Especially since I don't have anything else planned."

"Why are we stopping here?" Jan asked as her father swerved into a strip mall.

"Do you guys feel like having a roti?" He pulled up on a concrete pathway and reversed into the sole vacant parking spot.

"Yeah," Jan and Tamera answered, almost in unison.

"Well," Charlie said. "Get off your butts and come in the shop."

"No, Dad, I can't." Jan sniffed her armpits. "I smell like raw fish."

"I'm coming," Tamera said and unfastened her seatbelt.

"Bring me a beef roti." Jan reclined the front passenger seat and opened a book.

"Earl should have left for work by now, so I only buying one for your mom," Charlie said. He and Tamera stood in line, waiting to be served. "Should we get her beef too?"

"Ma had the runs the last time Mary bought her a beef one," Tamera smiled.

"This is the best roti shop in the world," he said. "I bet the one that made your mother ill wasn't purchased at this establishment."

"It's probably better to get her a vegetarian one," Tamera insisted. "'Cause if you buy her anything else, she may not want to eat it."

"Okay then," Charlie said.

"This is sooo good." Jan sat in the front passenger seat at an angle, so she could look over at Tamera as she too tackled her roti with appetite. "It's definitely the best roti I've ever tasted," Jan said, taking a second bite.

Charlie swerved out of the parking lot, leaving his and Alison's roti on the back seat. They would eat later. The girls gulped down their meal, and after they were finished, they admired the lush scenery rushing past them on the drive home.

"We're almost home." Charlie turned off the highway, and continued along a narrow road. He pulled aside for a vehicle travelling in the opposite direction to safely pass. "If the people who designed these roads had any foresight, they'd have made these roads a bit wider to accommodate two-way traffic." He drove along the narrow road ten more minutes, and as he swung around the corner, a loud bang almost popped his and the girls' eardrums. Within seconds, another booming sound ruptured all around.

"That can't be firecrackers!" Jan covered both ears with her hands.

"We're gonna soon find out." Charlie steered the vehicle at a steady pace until they could come to a stop safely.

"Look over there!" Tamera pointed to plumes of billowing black smoke rocketing toward the sky.

"Where there's smoke, there's got to be fire," Jan said.

"It's got to be pretty close to the water," Charlie said as bits of black ash rained down on the windshield. By the time he drove past La Cresta Primary School, dense smoke had completely engulfed the sky. Charlie stopped the car at the top of Jonko Trail. Many villagers were already making their way along the rough dirt road. "What's on fire?" he asked, sticking his neck out the window.

"The fishing depot!" someone yelled. "We're heading down there to see for ourselves."

There were two ways to get to the depot: the main road or Jonko Trail, but the trail wasn't accessible to vehicular traffic, so Charlie parked the car on a grassy area. "You girls can walk home from here," he said as he jumped out of the vehicle. The girls climbed out too, and he secured the doors before heading over to join the men gathered on the beach.

"See you later, 'cause I'm heading to the depot with everyone else," Jan said and waved at Tamera.

"I'm coming too," Tamera chimed, joining her uncle and cousin.

"Thought you were tired," Jan said.

"Not anymore," Tamera said. "The bang woke me up, and now I have enough energy to fly." She flailed her arms up and down, imitating wings.

"You're too much," Jan said, giggling.

The girls and Charlie found themselves in the middle of a growing crowd. The horn of a fire engine released a big, bold sound. None of them could see the gigantic red vehicle because a hill obstructed their view of the fisherman's depot and the paved road leading to it.

It took another ten minutes for them to get to the fire. "It's all gone." Charlie's face turned blood red as he watched the firemen aimed their hoses at the flaming debris. Tamera instantly recognized her father among three injured men lying on their backs on an uneven grassy spot. His two helpers, Clyde and Joshua's nephew, Otis, were hovering over him. Tamera pushed her way toward her father as a voice shouted, "People, stand back and let the firemen do their job."

Charlie and Jan looked on as Earl writhed in pain. He groaned and Tamera gasped. Her heartbeat raced like a hummingbird's when she noticed the large wound on her father's leg. Paramedics jumped out of an ambulance and flocked to him before attending to the others. They worked together to lift Earl onto a stretcher. Earl grimaced and contorted his lower limbs as they wheeled him into the emergency vehicle.

Clyde consoled Tamera while Otis stood next to Charlie and Jan, describing what he'd witnessed. As the ambulance pulled away, they spotted Alison and Renwick who were running towards Tamera.

"Where's your father?" Alison breathed as heavily as if she'd just crossed the finish line of a long-distance race. Mary was was just behind Renwick. She was holding her pregnant belly as she panted and looked around hoping to spot Earl.

"Dad's in the ambulance," Tamera explained. "The paramedics are taking him to the hospital. He has a bad gash on his leg."

"My car is at the top of Jonko Trail, so I've got to make it back there. I'll meet you folks at the hospital," Charlie said.

"I'm going to take you straight there," Renwick said, taking Alison's hand.

"I'm coming too." Tamera coughed as the burned-out structures continued to spew out clouds of thick black smoke that enveloped them.

"I'm going with my dad," Jan said and followed her father back to his car.

Many fishermen looked on helplessly; some were in tears. The fire had started at Shed Four and spread to all the storage and mending sheds. "It's real weird that there's a big ocean right here and the buildings are all gone," Renwick frowned. Tamera and Alison nodded in agreement, then climbed into his vehicle along with Mary, leaving Clyde and Otis behind.

The inhabitants of La Cresta later learned that someone had carelessly disposed of a cigarette, which had ignited when a fisherman was siphoning gas from a container. All the sheds and eight boats were burned. Ten fishermen also lost their nets.

Earl remained in the hospital for a week and came home on crutches. "I've gotta get back to work by the end of the month," he said two weeks after his discharge. He and Charlie were in the living room. They had just watched a Saturday afternoon football match between Arsenal and Manchester United.

"Don't rush it," Charlie advised. "If you go back too soon, you're going to regret it."

Two fishermen who'd lost their boats in the fire asked Earl if they could use his vessel to ply their trade until he was fit enough to return to work. He wasn't too keen at first, but after a lengthy discussion with Charlie, he agreed. Alison was happy about this arrangement because it brought in some cash, so that she and Earl didn't have to dip into their savings while he was convalescing.

At times, Earl would sit on the porch for hours in silence, barely responding when anyone spoke to him. On other occasions, he vehemently expressed his frustration over his leg, which he didn't think was healing as swiftly as it should. Three weeks after returning home from the hospital, he was still hobbling around on crutches. That same week, Mr. Joshua asked him if Tamera could help out at his shop for two weeks because his wife was scheduled to have minor surgery.

"If she wants to, it's not a problem with either me or my wife," Earl said.

Since Tamera needed cash, she agreed to help on the condition that she'd have the Independence Weekend off to head to Port City to watch the parade with Jan and her mom.

But when that weekend arrived, Tamera changed her mind. "I'm not going to bother to go to Jan's place for the weekend," Tamera said as she stood next to her mother's bed just after midday on Friday. She was having second thoughts about leaving La Cresta for the entire long weekend. Her mother had seemed listless for the past couple of days, and that morning, Tamera thought she looked pale.

"No," Alison said. "You must go to Port City. I'm going to be all right."

"But you don't look like yourself," Tamera said, her voice edged with concern.

"I'm telling you that I'm going to be fine, and I mean it," Alison insisted.

"Ma? You're sure 'bout that?"

"Your sister's next door," Alison scowled. "I don't know what you're so worried for."

"Okay, Ma. Then I'll go." Tamera planted a loud kiss on her mother's cheek and went to her room to pack a few belongings.

That afternoon, for the first time since his accident, Earl planned to drive to the fishing depot to head out to sea with the fishermen to whom he'd loaned his boat. He was going to take full control of his vessel the following week, and his helpers, Clyde and Otis, had already agreed to return to work for him.

"Bye, Dad," Tamera said, waving at her father just before he turned onto Chester Street. She shut the front gate behind her and walked toward Charlie's car, which was parked as usual in front of his house.

"You're ready to hit the road?" he asked. Tamara smiled and nodded, and they sped off toward Port City.

Jan and her mother lived in a nine-storey apartment building bordered by large, red hibiscus and tall bushes of white and pale pink roses. Jan met her dad and Tamera at the entrance. "You're okay?" Charlie embraced his daughter. They chatted for a few minutes, and after exchanging pleasantries, Charlie left. Jan carried Tamera's duffle bag onto the elevator.

The girls entered a fifth-floor apartment with a cozy balcony to the right of the main door. "Good to have you visit," Jan's mom greeted her.

Later that afternoon, Tamera and Jan sat on the balcony that had an excellent view of the city. "Mom doesn't need a car here," Jan said. "It takes her less than ten minutes to walk to work, and to get to school it takes me only five minutes longer than her."

When Dalton's number popped up onto her phone, Tamera eagerly answered. Dalton was in Barbados with his friends for the long weekend. "We're waiting for our lift to take us to the hotel," he said.

"You had a good flight?"

"Yeah, except that my ears feeling a bit cloggy."

"Mrs. Joshua said that people chew gum on the plane to prevent that."

"That didn't totally work for me," he said. "You're in Port City right now?"

"Yeah, I'm at Jan's place."

"Looking forward to the parade?"

"It's better than staying home and doing nothing."

"We're heading to Crane Beach on the South Coast of the island. That's where me and my posse plan to spend the entire weekend."

"You spent all that money to go to Barbados just to hang out by the beach? You could have done the same at home, and you wouldn't have had to spend a red cent."

"The same old, same old gets boring after a while. It's important to try something different sometimes."

"Is that why you only come home once a month now?" Tamera asked, a slight tremor in her voice.

"What does my coming home have to do with my trip to Barbados?"

"You said it's important to try something different, otherwise it gets boring. Do you think I'm boring, and that's why you hardly come home anymore?"

"Hold it!" He paused. "Is it really my Tammy who's talking? My friends have those sorts of problems with their girls, but me and you are supposed to be above that."

"You can't be mad that I'm thinking this," Tamera said. "I miss your visits."

"Who's putting these ideas in your head?"

"I have a brain, and I can think for myself. I don't see you enough, and that's a problem in any relationship."

"Now is a bad time to talk," he said. "I'll call you tomorrow."

The following morning, Jan, her mom, and Tamera made their way to the largest park on the island, located in the centre of the city to witness the Independence Day military-style parade. When they arrived at the park all the seats were taken, so they had to stand. The feeling of patriotism filled the air and almost everyone, including Tamera, Jan, and her mother was dressed in red and blue, the country's national colours. Many people waved the national flag. Dignitaries, including the prime minister, the president, and cabinet members made their way to the VIP section of the stands. The celebrations began with the performance of the national anthem by members of the police musical band. Other protective service organizations present included the island's Regiment, the Coast Guard, Fire Services personnel, and the Red Cross.

The prime minister and other dignitaries made grand speeches and His Excellency, President Jones, with a lot of pomp and ceremony inspected a guard of honour at the event. After the official activities at the parade grounds ended, the contingents marched through the streets to the accompaniment of live music by numerous military bands. Jan, her mom, and Tamera joined hundreds of jubilant spectators on the parade route. After the parade, they returned home and munched on the previous day's leftovers. After lunch, Jan's mother watched the National Awards ceremony where citizens of the island were presented with medals for having had a significant and positive impact on the island. Tamera stuck it out for the first ten minutes and then made her way to the porch. Jan followed her there about fifteen minutes later.

"Dalton's on vacation," Jan said. "Don't spend the entire afternoon moping because he didn't call you back yet."

"He'd better have a good excuse," Tamera pouted.

"You never questioned his honesty until Mary put those thoughts in your head," Jan said. "I've known Dalton as long as you have, and he's a good guy."

"You don't know everything 'bout him," Tamera paused. "He used to hassle me to send him photos in my underwear, and I think he's still upset that I refused to do it."

"He did that?" Jan's jaw dropped. "How come I don't know none of that?"

"It's a difficult topic to talk 'bout," Tamera said and lowered her head. She didn't tell Jan that she almost sent him the pictures he wanted, until Mary found out and shamed her.

Tamera dialled her father's cell phone one day before she planned to go home. Earl answered the call but didn't sound like himself. After a bit of prodding, he acknowledged that Alison wasn't doing too well. "Don't worry about your mom," he said. "She always bounces back no matter what."

Tamera's jaw stiffened as she hung up the phone.

"Pay attention to your surroundings and get off at Johnson's Mall. It's a big yellow building. You can't miss it." Jan's mother had taken Tamera to the Port City bus terminal.

"Okay," Tamera nodded, excited to be travelling on her own for the first time on a bus from the city.

"It's time for you to board," Jan's mom said when the bus arrived. "It was a pleasure having you here. You're welcome back anytime."

"Thanks so much for everything." Tamera boarded the bus, waving. She settled into a second-row window seat. She shut her gravelly eyes, regretting wasting precious time worrying about how much fun Dalton was having in Barbados and losing several hours sleep the previous night. An image of her mother in her birthday suit consumed her thoughts. She opened her eyes.

Charlie had promised to pick her up at Johnson's Mall, the mid-point between La Cresta and Port City. And since she'd never travelled solo by bus from the city, among the anticipation of doing something brand new was the apprehension that she might get lost. She tried to block out the noisy passengers, focusing instead on the approaching landmarks. She got off the bus at the prearranged spot but didn't see Charlie. Renwick was there instead of him.

She walked over to her brother-in-law who stood next to his car, his face tense, holding the phone to his ear. "Where's

Uncle Charlie?" she asked, worried that something bad had happened.

"He couldn't make it. He asked me to pick you up instead." Renwick put her luggage in the trunk. "Climb in." He held the door and closed it behind her after she had settled.

Heaviness filled her chest as she buckled her seatbelt, and noted the worry etched on his face. She wondered if he and her sister were having serious marital problems again.

"I'm tired like a dog," she said.

Renwick didn't say anything. He switched on the radio, and minutes later she dozed off.

"Tammy," Renwick was gently tapping her on the shoulder. "It's time to get up."

"We're home already?" She lifted her head and opened eyes, surprised that La Cresta Elementary School was on her left.

"I've gotta tell you something," he said softly.

"What?"

"I-I," he stuttered. "I-I've got to tell you—" His face sagged.

"You're scaring me," she whispered and rubbed her palms together.

He lowered his head, refusing to look her in the eyes. "Your mom. S-s-she's missing."

"Missing?"

"They're out looking for her," he said. "Your dad, Mr. Charlie, Mr. Joshua, the rest of the neighbours, everybody."

"You're joking, right?" She clasped her hands together, and twisted her fingers nervously.

"Tammy, it's true."

"Stop playing games with me."

"I'm real sorry, Tammy," Renwick said, his eyes tearing up.

"Why nobody didn't call me?"

"Your mom's been missing only this morning. It would have made no sense to tell you on the bus."

Tamera started crying and frantically searched for her phone. "I've gotta talk to Pa," she sobbed.

"Don't worry, they're going to find her," he said. "Let me drive you home."

She dialled her dad's phone number, her hands shaking violently. After seven rings, the call went to voicemail. She punched in Mary's number, but she didn't answer either.

Renwick's phone rang. "Yes, okay," he said to the caller and quickly hung up.

"That was your Uncle Charlie," he said.

"They found Ma?" she said.

"Not yet." Renwick parked in front of Tamera's home. "Mary's at your parents' place. Tell her I went to help with the search." He remained in the driver's seat, staring at Tamera as she jumped out the car and darted up the staircase.

"Mary," Tamera yelled, beating on the front door with her fist. Renwick drove off just as his wife unlocked the door.

"Tammy." Mary embraced her sister. "I'm so glad you're here."

"Ma's really missing?" Tamera's voice cracked.

Mary nodded.

"Renwick told you 'bout the money?"

"No," Tamera replied. "I don't know nothing 'bout that."

Mary held her sister's hand. "Come let me tell you what's going on." They sat down next to each other on the three-seater sofa, and Mary gripped her sister's hand tighter.

"The day before yesterday, Ma spent all the money Pa set aside for bills on lottery tickets, and when Pa realized that the money was gone, he got really mad. And to calm himself down, he cuffed the wall real hard, hurting his fingers. Then yesterday, Ma picked a fight with Pa just because he switched television channels. And she wasn't even in the room when he did. Later in the day, she started to dance about the house swearing that she was God. You know how Ma behaves when she gets real hyper, so Pa didn't want her to stay here alone when he went out on the boat, so he asked me to come over. I checked on Ma before me and Emma went to sleep in my old room. I checked on Ma at one-thirty this morning, and again when I went to use the bathroom. At six this morning, she talked to me normal when I told her I was going home to get my charger because the battery on my phone was running low. I stayed over there about half an hour straightening up the place. When I reached back here, she wasn't in the bedroom, she wasn't in the house, and I couldn't find her nowhere. So, Pa, Uncle Charlie, and some of the neighbours are out looking."

"You called the police?" Tamera said.

"Of course, I called them," Mary said. "But they told me to come down there and give a statement."

"You went?" Tamera questioned.

"Yeah," Mary said. "I went down there with Uncle Charlie afterward."

"What are we gonna do?" Tamera said. "What if something bad happened to Ma?"

"No, Tammy," Mary said. "We've gotta think positive and believe that Ma's going to be okay."

The sisters hugged, tears streaming down both their faces. The home phone rang. "It's probably Pa," Tamera said and rushed across the room to grab the receiver.

"Is Mr. Telford's land still for sale?" said a female voice.

Tamera hesitated.

"Who's this?" She didn't recognize the name or number on the caller ID.

After a short silence, the caller identified herself as Michelle Edwards, the woman from Boston who months earlier had come to La Cresta with her husband to inspect the land Earl had put up for sale.

"Yes, it is," Tamera said. "Pa hasn't found a buyer yet."

"That's good for us, because we're still interested," the woman continued. "My husband had some major health issues, and our lives have been on hold, but his health has improved and we're ready to go ahead with the transaction."

Tamera explained that her father was not home right now and that he would have to call her back. The woman couldn't have picked a worse time to call, but Tamera didn't say anything about that.

She took the woman's number and walked back to the sofa, recalling how horrible she had felt when LaToya went missing. Now her mom was missing too. She was feeling ten times worse than the day she heard about LaToya.

The phone rang again. "It's Aunt Leila," Mary said, handing the phone to her sister.

"Aunty," Tammy sobbed, pressing the phone against her earlobe.

"I'm so sorry," Aunt Leila said. "I'm coming over. I should be there in under an hour."

Emma toddled into the living room, rubbing her eyes with the back of her hand. Mary made a peanut butter and jelly sandwich and gave it to her. "Do you want one?" She looked across at Tamera with the butter knife in her hand.

"No, I'm not hungry," Tamera said.

Emma ate her sandwich and licked her fingers clean. "You're finished?" Mary said. Emma nodded. Mary picked up the plate but pivoted when she heard voices in the yard.

Earl walked up the staircase ahead of Charlie and Joshua and entered the living room. His brother and friend remained on the porch. "Where's Ma?" Mary asked and hurried toward her father.

Tamera ran to him and clung to his arm. "Pa?"

He squeezed Tamera's right hand, keeping his eyes on the ground. "Pa?" Her voice quivered.

He lifted his head slowly. "Girls," he said in a timid whisper. "I'm real sorry to bring bad news, but girls, your mother's gone." His hands shook and his voice quavered. "Her body washed up on the shore."

"No!" Tamera dashed across the room, heaving. "Ma can't

be dead, she can't be gone! She's going to come through that door! She's got to!"

Earl walked slowly toward his younger daughter, and embraced her, trying to comfort her. But he was devastated and he couldn't hold back his own tears.

"If I didn't go to Port City, Ma would have been alive!" Tamara cried and covered her face with both hands

"It's nobody's fault," Earl said, wiping his eyes with a tissue. "It was an accident."

Tamera's face looked up at him, her face as white as a ghost's.

"Somebody bring her something to drink," Earl said.

Mary scurried toward the kitchen, returning with a glass of water. Earl led Tamera to the sofa. "Take a sip," he said and pressed the glass against Tamera's lips. She swallowed a mouthful and then shoved his hand away. "I don't want no more."

Silent tears flowed down Mary's face as she sat next to her sister, her arm wrapped around her shoulders, holding her close. They were all in shock.

"I'm here," Renwick said, bursting through the front door. He tried to hug his wife, but her face was buried in Tamera's neck.

Mary and Tamera clung to each other. Earl's eyes darted toward the doorway as LaToya's mom, Cynthia, followed Renwick inside. "Please accept my condolences," she said, looking grim.

"Thanks so much for coming." Earl shook his head, walking toward her. "This is life," he said.

"I'm real sorry you all lost your mother," Cynthia grimaced, her eyes on the sisters. "I understand what you all are going through," she said.

LaToya was still missing. Almost five months had passed and there were still no credible leads regarding her whereabouts. The villagers rarely discussed LaToya anymore, but her mother's pain lingered on.

The girls sobbed and nodded, as they each hugged her back.

# 19.

JAN PHONED TAMERA THE NEXT DAY. "How you doing?" Jan said as Tamera picked up the receiver.

"Everything's so hard right now," Tamera sobbed. "I don't think I'll ever get over losing my mom."

"I wish there was something I could do to cheer you up," Jan said softly. "But I don't know what to do."

"There isn't anything anybody can do," Tamera said.

Jan wasn't sure how to respond, so for a while she remained silent, listening anxiously as Tamera cried. "I'll check on you later today," she eventually said.

"Okay," Tamera said, hanging up. She wiped the tears streaming down her cheeks with the back of her hand. Moments later, the phone rang again. It was Dalton.

"Hi, Tammy," Dalton said. "How are you?"

"Why are you asking?"

"Because you're my girl and I want to make sure you're okay." She remained silent.

"Tammy?"

"What?"

"You don't sound like yourself. You're sure you're okay?" he paused. "I hope you're not mad at me."

"I have good reason to be."

"Sorry for not calling before, but things turned really ugly in Barbados," he said. "Our driver got hit from behind, and then the police arrested him for failing a breathalyzer test."

"Your driver was drunk?"

Dalton chuckled. "He was a little over the limit. It was a crazy time. And it spoiled the entire weekend."

"When are you coming home?"

"In two weeks," he said. "And I promise you I'm not going to cancel that trip."

"You're not coming for the funeral?"

"Funeral?" he said. "What are you talking 'bout, Tammy?"

"You're coming home for the funeral or not?" Tammy persisted.

"Stop talking in riddles. I don't know what you're talking 'bout?"

"My mother," Tamera paused. "She died yesterday morning."

"You're serious?" he said. "What happened?"

"They have to do an autopsy before we know for sure."

"How come you didn't call me?"

"I thought your mom or dad would tell you."

"I'm real sorry, but no one told me nothing. My parents probably thought you already phoned me." He sighed loudly. "I'm going to talk to my boss when I hang up and ask for time off to come to the funeral, okay?"

Villagers gossiped that Alison probably killed herself, but the post-mortem autopsy stated that she died of accidental drowning. Her younger sister, Leila, took charge of the funeral arrangements. Mourners attended in respectable numbers, even though the service took place on the first day of the new school term.

Dalton remained at Tamera's place for almost three hours after the funeral, although he repeated several times that he didn't want to get back to San Pedro too late." He kept checking the time on his cell phone, rising to his feet impatiently, then sitting back down again.

When it was finally time for Dalton to leave, Earl shook his hand and thanked him for coming.

"It was important for me to be here," Dalton said. "Pop's always talking so highly of you. It's really sad what your family's going through, and I really wish there was something more I could do."

"Don't worry," Earl said. "We're going to get over this in time."

Dalton trudged down the staircase and Tamera followed, shielding her eyes from the glare. They stood facing each other in front of Dalton's fiery-red car, staring at each other, and holding hands. As Tamera's tears flowed, he wiped her moist face with his fingers, then kissed her on the cheek, delicately squeezing her fingers.

"Call me when you get to San Pedro, okay?" she said.

"Will do." He slid into the driver's seat and shut the door. She arched forward, positioning her elbows on the rim of the front window. He kept his eyes on her face, while his right hand searched for the handbrake. He clutched its tip and she backed away moments after he lifted it. "Goodbye," he waved, smiling softly. Her lips curved a little. He throttled the car from the curb, and she frowned as it vanished around the corner.

When Tamera headed to the bathroom the following morning, her legs felt as if they were supporting a six-hundred-pound woman. She trudged from the toilet to her bed and remained there most of the day, barely eating anything.

Two days later, Mary pulled the covers off her sister. "Come on, Tammy. Get out of bed," she moaned. "I'm not leaving this room until you take a shower and comb your hair."

Tamera rolled from her stomach to her back. She sat upright, propping herself with two fluffy pillows. "I'm missing Ma too, you know," Mary said. "Losing her is more than enough, and I'm not gonna lose you too."

Tamera grudgingly shifted to the edge of the bed and slowly slipped off.

"Good." Mary handed her a green-and-white outfit. "Put this on when you finish bathing."

Tamera inspected the pretty dress but didn't say anything. It was new. Maybe Mary had bought it for her.

"Me and Renwick are gonna take you for a drive, and you're going with us whether you want to or not."

About half an hour later, Tamera stepped onto the porch. She scowled when she noticed Cynthia sitting on a chair next to her father.

"That's a pretty dress you have on," Cynthia said.

"Thanks," Tamera mumbled.

"Get some fresh air," Earl said, a wide smile on his face. He placed his hand gently on her arm and looked at her encouragingly. "Glad you're going out."

"See you guys later," Mary said, and marched down the staircase; Tamera lumbered after her.

"Come on," Mary said impatiently, but Tamera continued to walk slowly, inhaling the honeyed scent of freshly cut grass.

"Why's she always here?" Tamera asked when they got to Renwick's car.

"You're talking 'bout Cynthia?"

"Who else is always at our house since Ma died?" Tamera scowled.

"She and Dad go way back, and he needs someone to cheer him up, so we can't complain 'bout that."

"What about her big ugly tattoos and the ring in her nose that you always used to complain about."

"Cynthia is a big woman, and Pa is a big man. It's not as if he's going to marry her. They're both grieving. They're helping each other deal with their pain."

"You always used to criticize her skimpy clothes."

"Tammy," Mary said. "You of all people know that since LaToya's been missing, Cynthia don't dress like that no more."

"You're strange," Tamera pouted.

"Me. Strange?"

"Yes, you," Tamera paused. "You used to bad talk Cynthia all the time, and now you're behaving as if you and she are friends."

A few weeks after the funeral, Earl had closed the land deal on the property he had been trying to sell for months. "That's a weight off my chest," he'd said, putting his briefcase on the hardwood floor. The next day, he handed Tamera five one-hundred-dollar bills. "Take this," he said gruffly. "Buy yourself some new clothes and go out and have fun with your friends."

"Thanks, Pa," Tamera said, surprised but pleased. She slid the money into her wallet then sat at the edge of her bed, waiting for her dad to say something else.

Earl was looking at her expectantly. "It's breaking my heart to see you moping around the house like this," he said as he sat on the bed next to her.

"You don't need to worry, Pa," Tamera smiled half-heartedly. "I'm going to be all right. All I need is time."

"I'm glad to hear you say that," Earl's expression lightened as he got up. "Your mother wouldn't be happy to know that you're wasting your life moping in your room."

After Earl stepped out her room, Tamera climbed off her bed and trailed to the window, staring out at the brick wall that the window faced on. The new property owners had hastily constructed the wall immediately after they purchased the land. It was surrounded by an iron gate secured by a thick chain. Tamera would have preferred to look out at the empty lot than have this wall block her view. She ignored her phone, even though the caller ID displayed Jan's name. Earlier that day she'd also disregarded a call from Azura. She never doubted her two closest cousins' genuineness, but she resented the fact that, unlike her, they still had their mothers to cling to if they needed or wanted.

The following weekend, Tamera's friend, Cassandra, knocked

on her front door. "Wassuuuuuup?" she said when Tamera opened the door.

"What are you doing here?" Tamera said. It had been a while since they'd finished school and last seen each other.

"You're not answering your calls," Cassandra said. "So I didn't have no choice but to show up in person. You want to go to the beach on Saturday morning?"

"No," Tamera said firmly. "I don't feel like it."

"Why not?"

"My mother…" Tamera's voice trembled.

"Oh," Cassandra said, covering her mouth with her hand. She touched Tamera's arm. "I forgot … I mean … I … I didn't remember. Sorry."

"It's all right," Tamera said. "You don't have to feel bad about it."

"Tammy?" Cassandra started, then paused. "If I plan a get-together at my house next Saturday, are you going to come?"

"Maybe," Tamera shrugged.

Cassandra, Manisha, and Chloe, three of Tamera's former classmates, arrived at Cassandra's home on Saturday at about four in the afternoon. Within minutes, it began to rain. The girls dragged four chairs in a semi-circle onto the porch. Manisha and Chloe began talking about their mathematics teacher who was due to go on maternity leave the following month. "We're going to have to put up with another teacher for three whole months," Chloe said.

"I hope we get a good replacement," Manisha moaned.

"Me too," Chloe said."

"Please," Cassandra said. "You guys are boring Tamera. She doesn't know that teacher."

Shortly after the rain stopped, the girls walked down Chester Street. Manisha and Chloe were slightly ahead of Tamera and Cassandra. A car sped along the street and splashed muddy water up at them. They jumped away from the curb, barely escaping being soaked. "Let's cross over," Manisha whispered.

"That doesn't make any sense, 'cause we're going to have to cross back over when we get to the corner," Cassandra said with a puzzled expression.

"Don't you see who's coming up the street?" Manisha's teeth barely separated.

"Oh." Cassandra giggled when she noticed Samuel's brother, Edgar, heading toward them.

"Come on, you guys," Manisha dashed over to the adjacent pavement ahead of her friends.

"He's looking his usual drab self," Cassandra snickered. "He shouldn't be on the street where decent people have to pass."

The girls guffawed, except for Tamera.

"If his wife was alive, he wouldn't be so messed up," Tamera frowned. "You guys don't have no clue how hard it is to lose someone you love."

Tamera's friends transformed from animated objects to zombies. "Let's cross back," Cassandra said as they approached the corner of Chester Street. They nodded and waited for a gap in the oncoming traffic to cross to the other side.

"We were just having a little bit of fun, Tammy," Manisha said. "We didn't mean no harm."

Tamera bit her lip.

Dalton was one of only a few people with whom Tamera had kept in touch on a regular basis since her mother's death. He still visited La Cresta only once a month, but he phoned or texted her almost every evening. "Did you hear that the police found a bunch of girls in Carson who were being forced to work at a club?" he said.

"No," Tamera sat up, her interest piqued. "Where are they from?"

"South America," he said. "And the worst part is that some of them are not even eighteen yet."

"They arrested anyone?

"Three people. Two men and a woman."

"They should spend a long time in jail," Tamera said. "I sometimes wonder if some evil person is holding LaToya against her will and making her do horrible things."

"I know what you mean," he said. "Those girls were kept at that house way longer than LaToya's been missing."

Tamera headed down the staircase and to her sister's house after finishing her conversation with Dalton.

"What's your father doing?" Cynthia crossed paths with Tamera in the yard.

"He's watching television," Tamera said.

She and Cynthia didn't have a close relationship but were being civil to one other.

"Did you hear about the South American girls?" Cynthia had larger bags than normal under her eyes.

"Yeah," Tamera replied, then stood for a moment, wondering if she should say anything else. Instead, she turned around quickly and continued toward her sister's place.

Cynthia lit a cigarette. The smoke trailed her. She briskly walked up the staircase and knocked on the front door.

"You're good?" Earl stepped onto the porch.

"Trying to be." She hunched forward, tapping the cigarette onto the edge of a ceramic ashtray designed like a toilet bowl that she had brought to the house several days before. The ashes dropped in. She stood upright and took another puff with her eyes shut. She extracted the *Juniper Express* newspaper from her bag. "Here, check page two," she said as she handed Earl the newspaper and sank into a chair next to him. He flipped the page. His lips moved as he silently read the details about what had happened to the South American girls. "They must have gone through hell," she said, tears springing to her eyes. "I stayed up last night wondering if somebody's doing the same thing to my child."

# 20.

FIVE WEEKS AFTER ALISON'S PASSING, Tamera was curled up on her bed, reading a magazine.

"Tammy," Mary yelled from the kitchen.

She abandoned the magazine on her bed and trotted obediently to the kitchen. "What do you want?" she asked.

Charlie was sitting with his back slightly curled, facing Mary while Earl was pacing up and down the room, grimacing. "Uncle Charlie, I didn't know you were here," Tamera said.

"I just arrived," he grunted.

"What's going on?" Tamera said.

"There's an oil spill on the beach," Earl said.

"Our beach?" she grimaced, placing her right hand over her mouth.

"Yeah," Charlie said with a brittle laugh. "The beach is covered in oil."

"But that's going to destroy the environment and kill the wildlife," she said.

"And my livelihood," Earl said, walking toward her in a pair of short khaki pants. "I'm going down there to see the damage myself." A scar ran from his thigh to his calf, a reminder of the injury sustained during the fire.

"Wait for me," Tamera said and darted to her room. She slipped on a pair of shorts and a T-shirt and then pulled her hair into a ponytail, securing it with an elastic band. She made it back to the kitchen in under five minutes. "Where's Pa and

Uncle Charlie?" Tamera asked.

"They've gone outside," Mary said as Emma climbed on her lap, clutching a doll whose hair she had been combing with a toy brush.

"It smells." Tamera said, making a face. She placed an open palm against her chest as though she were holding the air in her lungs, then she walked toward the door and slipped on a pair of sneakers. Emma ran toward her and looked up at her with a big pout on her face.

"You can't go with me," Tamera said and shooed her away. "You've got to stay with your mom."

Emma wrapped her arms tightly around Tamera's leg and started to whimper. "Come and get her," Tamera said, looking across the room at Mary who was still sitting on the sofa, arms wrapped around her ever-expanding belly.

"Emma," Mary said gently, awkwardly pulling herself up. She waddled toward her daughter. "Tammy has to go now. You'll see her later."

Mary tried to coax Emma to release Tamera's leg, but the child held on tighter. She finally relented. "Okay," Mary smiled, "We'll go outside for a little while, but we can't stay there too long."

Tamera slipped on Emma's shoes and then held her hand as they walked down the stairs. Mary followed them, huffing laboriously as they made their way down the street.

"Yeah, it sure smells like oil," Mary said as traces of a pungent odour seeped up into her nostrils.

They walked silently along the pavement, joining Renwick, Earl, Charlie, and five other neighbourhood men who'd gathered in front of Charlie's house. "This is a real nightmare," Earl said.

"How could the so-called experts let this happen?" Samuel asked.

"The authorities better act quickly and figure out the source of the problem," Joshua said. "'Cause we don't want to hear about another oil leak in a neighbouring community next week."

Emma tried to escape from her aunt's grasp. "No," Tamera admonished her niece, clutching her wrist a little tighter. A panel van zoomed by, leaving behind a trail of smelly exhaust.

"I'm not feeling good at all," Mary said and propped herself against Renwick's arm. "This is probably not good for the baby," she added. Minutes later, he led his heavily pregnant wife and daughter home.

"Charlie and me going down to the beach right now," Earl announced.

Samuel looked at his phone. "I've got to pick up my son and I'm already running late." He crossed the street, climbed into his car and drove off.

"My friend, Malcolm's coming to look at my broken washing machine, so I can't head to the beach until later today," Joshua said, and walked away.

"I'll take a cool walk over there," Harold, who also lived on Chester Street, said.

"We can walk together," Nathan, his next-door neighbour suggested.

"Good idea, but I've got to go home and put on proper shoes." Harold glanced at his flip-flops.

"I'll go with you all," Joseph, Harold's brother said.

As some of the other men dispersed, Earl turned to his family, who had gathered beside him. "You're sure you really want to go down there?" Earl said as Tamera climbed into Charlie's car.

"Pa, I'm going to be okay," she said.

"You're sure 'bout that?" Earl pivoted around, gauging her expression.

"Yeah, Pa," she smiled tenderly. "I'm ready."

Renwick and Mary decided to take their own car, leaving Earl and Tamera with Charlie. Charlie started the car and then swerved left, heading away from the beach.

"Uncle Charlie, where are you going?" Tamera asked, not sure why he was going in the opposite direction.

"To pick up Cynthia," Earl answered.

As soon as they arrived in front of her home, Cynthia hurried out the door and climbed into the car next to Tamera. "You're good?" Cynthia asked, patting Tamera's arm.

"Yeah," Tamera said, staring at Cynthia's garden, where chickweed, rattle weed, wild hops, and other unwanted plants had encroached on the once immaculate garden.

Charlie did a three-point turn, and waved at Dalton's father, who was sitting on his porch. He drove at a steady pace and parked within feet of the water. Tamera sensed her mother's presence, and a wave of sadness engulfed her. When Earl, Charlie, and Cynthia climbed out of the car, a strong punch of the gassy odour hit her nostrils again.

Tamera gritted her teeth, staying put in her seat.

"You're not coming out?" Earl said, noticing his daughter's odd expression.

"Yeah," Tamera said, trying to purge the sudden fear from her thoughts. She climbed out of the car moments later and joined the group.

"Let's go," Earl said, walking slightly behind Charlie but ahead of Tamera and Cynthia.


"This is it," Charlie glowered when they got to the sticky black shoreline, and even though he had forewarned his companions about the extent of the disaster, they weren't prepared for what they encountered. The gassy air stung Tamera's eyes, nose, and throat. It entered her lungs, and she almost choked. She covered her nose with her hands, but it barely eased her discomfort. She took a sip of water; it somewhat relieved her tickling throat.

About twenty slack-jawed villagers were standing at the far end of the beach examining the black sand, the debris that had washed onto the shore, and the oily sheen on the water. They were somewhat consoled when a group of oil company personnel wearing facemasks and white coveralls made their way onto the beach and began to assess the damage.

"It's frightening just to imagine what the oil did to our boats," Earl groaned.

"I can easily drive the car over there," Charlie said. "We can go and look for ourselves."

"No, let's take the short cut. My legs can handle it." Earl walked alongside his brother, and they moved steadily over the weeds. Tamera lingered behind, wishing to awaken from the nightmare.

They joined a group of fishermen and curious onlookers at the fishing depot, all of whom had their eyes fixed on the thick oil coating the fishing boats and nets.

A tall, lean man looked despairingly at Earl and his companions "We suffered in the fire, and now this."

"I saw the oil making its way to the shore. It happened so quickly. There wasn't time to do nothing," a man in a green cap said, his arms crossed tightly against his chest.

Earl stared at his oil-soaked boat, his eyes as wide as an owl's. It was anchored in shallow water next to the other vessels. The two sheds, rebuilt after the fire, were also saturated with the black oil.

"We're waiting for the clean-up crew to remove the sludge so we can get a closer look," said Bogo, the owner of one of the boats covered in oil. He and the other shell-shocked fishermen and their families mulled over what to do next.

That evening on the seven o'clock news, the minister of education announced that all schools in La Cresta would be closed until further notice. "We'll assess the situation and make a further announcement by the end of the week," he said.

Tamera, Charlie, and Earl returned to the shore the next morning. They watched as a cleanup crew released an absorbent along the shores and in the water. "They use it to stop the oil from spreading," Charlie explained. Tamera listened, and watched, in silence.

"Did you all see those crabs trapped in the black sludge?"

Charlie pointed to the crustaceans entombed in their oily graves. "They were probably in search of their nightly meal when they got caught."

Many species of birds were soaked in the black oil too, and Tamera couldn't take her eyes off a pelican covered in the oil that was barely alive. She didn't know what to do.

By the end of the second day following the oil spill, Emma's skin started to break out. Her mother also suffered from regular bouts of vomiting. Some of the other villagers complained of respiratory problems, and like Emma and Mary, many developed a variety of health problems.

A representative from Petro Oil Company warned the villagers not to have any open fires, and since gas was the sole fuel the residents used for cooking, no one was able to prepare a hot meal. The oil company promised to provide the community with food for as long as needed, but in the days that followed, the sole meal provided to them didn't arrive at their doorsteps until after six-thirty each evening.

"I don't know if they're telling us the truth," Joshua said after a spokesman for the oil company stated that the La Cresta spill bore no relationship to the earlier Carson River spill.

"There's no way the ordinary man can tell for sure," Earl shrugged.

Petro Oil Company also offered free medical care to the ailing residents. The doctors assigned to treat the villagers took their blood pressure and gave them prescriptions depending on their symptoms.

"Offering them medical care is a good step, but the most vulnerable residents should be immediately relocated," Joshua stated adamantly to a visiting television reporter.

Days later, the authorities announced that pregnant women and families with ailing children would be temporarily relocated to a government-owned apartment building. Charlie borrowed

Earl's van to transport some of Mary and Renwick's things to their temporary home. Tamera travelled to the housing complex in her father's vehicle, and Renwick's family went with him.

Mary's temporary home was on top of the steep hill that Tamera and her relatives had driven past on the way to see the leatherback turtles months earlier. Charlie firmly held the steering wheel as he drove cautiously up the hill. Tamera stared at her sister's temporary residence just ahead. "Mary's not going to be happy," Tamera said out loud.

"At least her health won't be compromised," Charlie said. "Sometimes we gotta be thankful for the little things in life."

Mary's face fell as she stepped out of her husband's car. "I guess this is home for now." She and Emma walked slightly ahead of Tamera, making their way along a crooked concrete pathway. "I hope we don't have to stay here too long," she moaned. Tamera stepped in front of her sister. A graffiti-ridden wall faced them.

"Hmmm." Mary sighed on entering the tiny box of a room. Emma tottered from one bedroom to the next, exploring the unfamiliar surroundings, while Renwick and Charlie lugged the furniture inside. Tamera unpacked a box of kitchen utensils. "Do you want me to put the plates in this cupboard or that one?" she said. Mary pointed to her left, trying to keep an eye on Emma as she scurried from the living room to the kitchen.

Renwick was scheduled to work the evening shift, and since Mary preferred not to spend her first night in unfamiliar surroundings with only Emma, she'd asked Tamera to spend the night. The living room felt stuffy and Mary could hardly breathe. Tamera adjusted a standing fan so that her sister could cool down, but they all had to contend with the awfully loud sound the fan was making. While Emma played with her toys, the sisters tried to watch television, but the noisy fan was a distraction. They didn't have access to cable television, and the few local channels didn't keep their interest, so they turned off the television and chatted primarily about the oil spill. By ten that evening they were all in bed.

Tamera awoke very early the following morning and took the bus home.

"Good morning, folks," Tamera said as she walked up the stairs to the porch.

"Good morning." Cynthia's right hand was spread over her chin, revealing nails eaten to the nub. She was sitting in the chair next to Tamera's dad.

"Morning, darling." Earl looked weary.

"You're okay, Pa?" Tamera dropped her duffel bag onto the terrazzo floor.

"Okay," he smiled weakly, informing her about a village meeting that had been hastily organized by Charlie and Joshua. "We're going to walk to the beach from the empty lot at the corner of Chester Street," he said. "We expect media people to meet us there."

That afternoon, when Tamera arrived at the beach with the other villagers, the reek of rotting fish was too strong for her bare hands to prevent from reaching her nostrils. She pulled a rag from her pocket, shielding her nose from the smell.

"Here," Charlie said when he noticed her, and handed her a facemask.

"Can I get one too?" Cynthia asked.

"Of course." Charlie extracted another one from a rectangular box and gave it to her. He shared the rest with some of the other villagers that had shown up.

"Petro Oil Company claims to have capped the leak and cleaned the beach," Charlie said to the growing crowd, "but look at the thick oil that's settled on the water again." His eyes flew from the shore to a flock of ravens feasting on dead moonshines, mullets, and other species of fish. "Believe me," he continued, "it's a holocaust for the wildlife here. The animals are oil-slicked and dying by the thousands."

Joshua stepped out from among the crowd. "The fish are

dying," he said. "The poison that's killing them is surely going to kill us too."

A cameraman focused his lens on fumes escaping from under the seabed. "This disaster's going to destroy our livelihood for good," Earl said when the reporter standing next to the cameraman requested a fisherman's opinion.

"We've gotta help ourselves and start cleaning this place up," Joshua said forcefully as the crowd began to disperse. Some villagers ignored his appeal and continued home; others began gathering the decomposing fish in large heaps. But before they were done, the high tide washed even more carcasses ashore.

The next day, the villagers took to the street after the oil company hired a clean-up crew consisting entirely of individuals from outside of La Cresta. "It's total disrespect to hire only outsiders to remove the dead birds and fish," Joshua said and held up a crudely made placard that read, "La Cresta people need jobs. We have rights too."

Tamera pressed the phone to her ear, confiding in Jan that she'd experienced a bout of diarrhea the previous evening. "Why don't you take the bus and come to Port City for a couple days?" Jan said.

"But you're already back at school," Tamera said. "It's going to be really boring for me to stay at your place past the weekend."

"I don't get home that late," Jan said. "And while me and mom are out, there's a whole lot you can do by yourself, like window shopping, visiting the museum, the gardens, or the zoo. You can also take a walk up to the savannah if you want to."

At first Tamera turned down Jan's offer, but when a rash appeared on her upper arm the following evening and later spread to her chest, her father encouraged her to accept the invitation.

# 21.

AT FIVE O'CLOCK ON FRIDAY afternoon, Tamera arrived at Jan's place. "I'm glad Renwick gave you a lift," Jan said. As she led Tamera to the bedroom, she added, "I'm really sorry that almost everything seems so crappy right now."

Tamera unzipped her charcoal duffel bag and fished out a change of clothing. On the way to Port City, she had tried not to focus on the oil spill but she couldn't get the dead fish that continued to wash ashore out of her thoughts.

"I'm sooo happy that you and Dalton patched things up," Jan smiled.

"Would you believe we've kept in touch every single day since Ma died?"

"That's cool."

"Yeah," Tamera said. "I couldn't bring myself to stay mad with him, even though the excuse he gave for not calling me back while he was in Barbados wasn't good."

"Don't worry," Jan patted her cousin's arm. "You did the right thing."

On Saturday morning, Earl phoned Tamera and told her more about the challenges the residents of La Cresta were facing. He filled her in regarding the variety of ailments the villagers were experiencing, their fear of contracting cancer due to the toxic air, and his concern for the survival of the ecosystem if the oil wasn't cleaned up properly. Earl also spoke about his distrust of those in authority. "This disaster's going to have a crippling effect on the fishing industry," he sighed. The despair in his voice tugged at her heart.

Afterward, Tamera tried to relax on the porch, soothing the rash that had spread to her neck with calamine lotion. She fervently wished she had the power to make the problems in her beloved birthplace vanish. Thinking about her mom made her slump in her seat and a tear trickled down her face.

"Why are you sitting out there moping?" Jan stepped onto the porch. "Let's go for a walk."

"Look at my skin," Tamera said and raised her blotchy arms so that Jan could clearly see the severity of the outbreak. She lifted her head, exposing the blemishes on her neck. "I'm not the only person from La Cresta with messed-up skin due to the oil spill. The fish and birds are dying, and it's not good for the environment," she continued. "Pa told me that one of the chemicals the oil company's using to remove the oil from the water is causing the animals to die, and nobody's taking responsibility for what's going on."

"There's nothing you can do 'bout that," Jan shrugged. "So why waste precious time sulking?"

"'Cause it's a big deal," Tamera's voice cracked. "The 'no fishing' and 'no bathing' signs on the beach are going to be there for a long time, and Pa and the other fishermen can't make a living."

"Tamera's right." Jan's mother stepped onto the porch. "We shouldn't ignore the hardships the villagers are facing just because we don't have an immediate solution to the problem."

On Monday morning, Jan spun around in her neatly ironed white blouse and red, white, and blue plaid skirt as if she were parading down a runway. "How am I looking?"

"Good," Tamera said, propping herself upright on the bed with two fuzzy pillows and positioning a third below her knees.

"That's it?" Jan giggled. She didn't notice Tamera's sad expression. "I thought I was more than just good!" Jan examined her image in a full-length mirror, fingering a zit on her cheek, but she didn't squeeze it. "It's a wonderful morning." She left the room with a big smile, adjusting her tie.

"Tammy, don't remain indoors all day. Make sure you get some fresh air," Jan's mother popped her head inside the bedroom.

"Okay," Tamera said, getting out of bed. She made her way to the kitchen, where Jan and her mother were preparing to eat breakfast. "I'm not hungry," she said when Jan's mother offered her some whole wheat bread, sausages, and cocoa tea.

"I'll be back around three-thirty," Jan said, pulling on a pair of white sneakers. "There's a lot to eat in the fridge. Help yourself to anything you want." Jan's mother opened the front door, ushered her daughter out, and then closed it with a loud thump. Tamera strolled onto the porch, and looked down at the concrete pathway that led to the street. Jan turned right at the gate, and her mother turned left, immediately blending in with the bustling crowd. Tamera wondered how she was going to keep herself busy until they got back.

She decided to take a quick shower. After that she stepped out the front door but didn't feel like walking very far. She had a quick look around the block and returned to the apartment a few minutes later. She powered on Jan's laptop and began to play the typing game. Her fingers were as stiff as an arthritic patient's, and she made more errors than normal. She was frustrated by her performance, so she logged out of the game. She tried to watch something on TV, but as she stretched to pick up the remote, the power went out. She thought about her mother and felt a cramping hollowness in the pit of her stomach. She threw her head down into a pillow and sobbed, tasting her tears.

"Tammy," Earl said on the phone. "You don't sound so good this morning."

"I'm okay, Pa," she lied.

But his voice had lost its spirit too. "I'm calling to tell you that more and more people here are getting sick. Things are so bad that even the mosquitoes are disappearing," he sighed. "It's best you stay put in Port City for a while longer."

Mary phoned Tamera at about eleven-thirty. "What are you doing?" she said.

"Sitting on the porch doing nothing, 'cause the power's gone. You're okay?" Tamera asked.

"Yeah," Mary said. "I'm going to take some tests today to make sure the baby's okay."

"You're taking the bus?" Tamera asked out of concern for Mary who was approaching her eighth month of pregnancy.

"No, Renwick's not working today, so he's going to take me there."

Tamera sighed with relief. "That's good," she said, nodding to herself.

"Did you hear from Pa today?" Mary asked.

"Yeah."

"What did he say?"

"That I should stay here for the time being, 'cause things are still bad in La Cresta, but I'm ready to go home."

"I know how you're feeling," Mary said. "I want to go home too. This place is really drab, and the people here don't have nothing better to do than minding other people's business." They talked for a while longer, but when Emma woke up, Mary had to end the call.

Tamera remained on the porch after talking with her sister, worrying about how many animals had lost their lives as a result of the oil spill. There was no way to know the precise figure, but she was certain it was in the millions.

"Did you eat?" were the first words Jan's mother uttered when she returned from work that afternoon.

"I had a peanut butter sandwich this morning," Tamera said.

"That's it?" Jan's mom didn't look too pleased.

"I wasn't hungry," Tamara responded.

"You can't survive on just that," Jan's mom said, shaking her head in disapproval. She strode into the kitchen and took several pieces of baked chicken and a container with rice and peas from the fridge. She warmed them in the microwave, filling the quiet space with a low, whirring sound.

"School was really good today," Jan said, sounding bubbly, as she slipped off her shoes at the door. She pulled off her tie and marched directly to her bedroom, without greeting either her mother or Tamera. Later she joined them at the kitchen table and gave them a quick review of her day.

Then she glanced at her mother pointedly. "How was work today?" she asked.

"Nothing extraordinary. I met a few clients in the morning and did a lot of paperwork in the afternoon."

"What about you, Tammy?" Jan said. "And please don't tell me you stayed in this boring apartment all day long."

"I walked two blocks and back."

"You didn't do anything else?" Jan stared at Tamera, her eyebrows raised in astonishment.

"No."

"Why not?" Jan shifted her gaze to the baked chicken on her plate and began slicing it.

"I needed time to think, 'cause I have some big decisions to make."

"Big decisions?" Jan lifted her head.

"I'm going back to school," Tamera said. She hadn't realized until that moment that she had made her decision. And that she now knew what she wanted to do.

"You're serious or just pulling my leg?"

"I'm not joking."

"That's the best news I've heard all week," Jan's mother said.

"You're going to redo math, I hope," Jan said.

"That and more," Tamera said. "I've been feeling so frustrated since the oil spill happened. I decided I want to help the people who're suffering back home, but I don't know what to do. I figured that if I get a good education, maybe I'll be able to make a difference."

"Don't tell me you want to be a lawyer," Jan said. "'Cause I can't see you doing that."

"Me. A lawyer?" Tamera pointed to her chest and smirked. "Never! I want to learn more about the environment. I think I want to study environmental science, and don't tell me I can't do it."

"I'm sure you can," Jan's mom said. "I'm so glad you found your passion."

Two weeks after Tamera arrived in Port City, she packed her possessions, readying herself for the journey back to La Cresta. "It's time for us to leave or you'll miss the next bus home," Jan's mother said, knocking on the bathroom door.

"I'll be out soon." Tamera checked her face in the mirror after applying ruby lipstick. She opened the door and walked toward Jan's bedroom. She zipped up her bag and placed it at the front door.

Just after one in the afternoon, they left for the bus terminal. "Call me as soon you arrive home," Jan's mother said, hugging Tamera.

"See you soon," Jan said. "And good luck with everything." She and Tamera embraced warmly. Tamera waved goodbye and then boarded the bus.

The journey to La Cresta took twice as long as normal due to a nasty collision between a car and a van. When Tamera finally climbed off the bus and started walking toward Chester Street, she was sweating profusely. She wiped her face and neck with a tissue and then scrunched it up in her hand. She felt the weight of her bag on her right shoulder, so she switched it to the left.

"The no-bathing signs are still on the beach," Charlie said as he watched his niece make her way up the staircase from his brother's porch. "So if you're thinking about taking a dip any time soon, forget about it."

"I talk to Pa every day," Tamera said, "and he keeps me posted on everything that's going on here."

As soon as she got up the stairs, Earl came out and embraced her. "Good to see you girl," he said.

"Hi, Pa." Tamera kissed her father's cheek. "I'm going to take a shower," she said and hurried to her bedroom. She phoned Jan's mother to let her know that she'd arrived home safely and then grabbed a towel and headed for the bathroom.

"Tammy!" Earl shouted about fifteen minutes later. "Show your face out here." His voice was much chirpier than it had sounded over the phone during the past two weeks.

"I'm coming, Pa." She changed into a pair of khaki shorts and a bright pink top and went back out to the porch. "Oh," she gasped, and stepped back. "I didn't know you were here."

"I just reached." Cynthia placed a tub of ice cream, a pink-and-white iced cake, and a stack of disposable plates, cups, and cutlery on the patio table.

"What are you all celebrating?" Tamera asked.

"You," Earl said.

"Me?"

"Your decision to go back to school." Charlie picked up a knife. "Let's cut this cake."

Schools in La Cresta reopened several days before Tamera returned home. And even though it was too late to register for CAPE classes, she contacted the school office to set up an appointment with the vice-principal. She thought it made sense to seek admittance to the evening CSEC mathematics class as a repeater with the hope that she would be allowed to register for CAPE classes the following year.

"I can fit you in to see Mrs. Summers at ten tomorrow morning," the secretary said. "Is that okay?"

"Thank you so much," Tamera beamed.

The La Cresta Secondary School building's bold curves and vertical lines attracted more eyes than any other structure in the tiny community. Tamera walked toward the front door, surprised that the formerly light-grey building was now slate grey. She arrived at the office more than half an hour before her scheduled meeting, and while waiting, she reminisced about her first day at secondary school. Back then, she wasn't much shorter, but she had definitely been skinnier.

"I'll see you now," said Mrs. Summers, the vice-principal, a tiny woman with a round face. She stepped out of her office, holding open the door.

"Thank you." Tamera entered the tidy office and sat primly on a green chair facing the vice-principal's desk.

"As you must be aware, it's too late to sign up for day CAPE classes, but since you were a student who always tried despite the challenges you've endured over the years, I'll make an exception and let you into the evening CSEC mathematics class," said Mrs. Summers. "If you want to join CAPE classes next year, make sure to submit your application on time," she warned.

"I sure will," Tamera said and smiled. She was ready.

# 22.

TAMERA WENT STRAIGHT HOME, and after changing into more comfortable clothes, she stepped into the backyard and began to pick up the clothes on the line that were flapping in the gusty breeze. She sighed, unable to escape the grinding noise coming from the neighbour's yard. Builders were in the midst of constructing a home on the land Tamera's father had sold to the Edwards. The level of noise the residents of Chester Street were made to endure depended on whether the builders were using concrete mixers, front-end loaders, backhoes, or some other piece of ear-splitting equipment. The steel frame of the unfinished building rose to the sky, confirming neighbourhood rumours that the house would have three storeys.

Tamera bundled the clothes in a large pile, and as she walked toward the back door, a large truck pulled up at the entrance of the unfinished home to deliver a fresh batch of materials. She stepped into her bedroom and folded the clothes into their respective piles. Afterward, she sorted her school books into two piles: the ones she was going to keep and those she was planning to get rid of. She was at home alone. Her father had accompanied Cynthia to the La Cresta Police Station to meet with the investigators in charge of her daughter's case.

*I can't deal with more bad news right now.*

Tamera tried to keep all negative thoughts out of her head. She put a book that she had used for her English Literature

CSEC exam on top of the pile she planned to get the rid of. She scanned through the pages of a thick hardcover mathematics book.

"I'm not going to let you frighten me no more," she said as she held the book to her chest, but when she heard her father's voice at the door, she abruptly dropped the book onto the bed.

"Pa?" She flew through the bedroom door.

"Well," he frowned, "the police found a body, so they're going to have to use dental records and possibly a blood test to see if there's a match."

"I see," Tamera said, quietly following her father to the kitchen, where Cynthia was sitting with her eyes shut and her arms tightly folded.

"I can't go on like this," Cynthia grimaced as she looked up at Earl. She took one sip from a glass of water and lowered her head into her hands.

Tamera left home at about five-thirty on Thursday afternoon to attend her mathematics class at La Cresta Secondary School. She entered the building, glancing at the admittance slip. She had arrived early and wasn't surprised to see only one student in the room. She sat ahead of the girl who had long, thick hair falling down her back. She'd recently begun to see this girl in the neighbourhood but didn't know her name. She looked at the admittance slip a second time, focusing on the teacher's name: *Mr. J. M. Thomas.*

By five minutes to six, fifteen people had taken their seats, and at exactly six o'clock, five more people shuffled into the room.

"He's late again," a man at the back of the room moaned.

"He's later than last Thursday." A man in the front row sucked his teeth.

"Please give him a break, he's a good teacher," the girl who'd arrived ahead of Tamera said.

"It don't matter," an older man said. "We suppose to start at six, and it already quarter past."

The room was hot with a discussion about the teacher's tardiness, and the women without exception were making excuses for him. By twenty past six, the noise in the room had escalated.

"Sorry, guys." The teacher's American accent caught Tamera off guard. She looked up, and unexpectedly caught his eyes. She lowered her head abruptly and fumbled with her mathematics textbook as she tried to open it. She was stunned that Samuel Thomas's nephew, Matthias, whom she had seen for the first time at the wire-bending exhibition months earlier, was at the front of the class taking attendance.

"Let's see who will solve this problem first." He neatly wrote out a mathematics problem on the white board.

The girl directly behind Tamera raised her hand and said, "I got it," then gave him the correct answer.

"That's really good," Matthias said. "Now let's try a few more."

At the end of the class, Tamera gathered her books, amazed at Matthias's brilliance. She threw her backpack over her shoulder and filed out of the room with her classmates. She turned left at the bottom of the staircase and walked along a concrete path, ignoring the convoy of vehicles leaving the school's circular parking lot. She didn't see anyone in front of her. She turned around and didn't notice anyone behind her either. Raindrops began to sprinkle her head and arms. She immediately regretted not bringing an umbrella. She tried to protect her hair with a book, but the rain started to come down heavier. "Oh no," she muttered, turning right on the sidewalk. An unfamiliar red car pulled up alongside her. "Climb in." A man's voice filtered out of the ruddy vehicle.

As he rolled down the window, Tamera saw that he had a big grin on his face. "I'm not going far," she said.

"I know that," Matthias said. "I'm staying at my uncle's house tonight, which is very close to your place."

She hesitated. "I don't mind walking."

"Come on," he said. "You'll get soaked, and then you'll be too sick to come to class."

She guardedly climbed into the seat next to him.

"I was surprised to see you tonight," he said, driving cautiously on the wet road. "How come you joined so late?"

"It's a long story, sir," Tamera said as rain drummed the windshield, and pelted the roof of the car.

"I'll be teaching the evening class for the next couple of months until your regular teacher gets back. So you'll definitely have time to tell me your long, long, story, even if it's on another day." He slowed down. "But it's a pity you can't tell me at least part of the tale today, 'cause you're already home." He pulled up in front of her house. "You can borrow mine," he said, handing her a colourful umbrella.

"Thanks, sir." She opened the door.

"Please don't call me sir. I'd rather you call me Matthias when we're not in class, okay."

Her teeth remained hidden as she smiled, opening the door.

She climbed awkwardly out of the car, opening the umbrella, and mistakenly set foot in a pool of water and slipped. The umbrella shifted sideways, allowing big drops of water to catch the back of her neck. She felt her face grow hot at the thought that Matthias had witnessed her clumsiness. She hurried up the staircase without looking back and as she reached the porch, she heard him drive away.

That evening, as heavy showers battered La Cresta, Tamera phoned Cassandra.

"Mr. Samuel's nephew is your teacher?" Cassandra said. "The one with the American accent?"

"Yeah," Tamera said. "You remember when we saw him at the wire-bending exhibition?"

"Of course. I remember that day as if it were yesterday," Cassandra said. "But it hurts when I think about LaToya."

"I know," Tamera said. "It's still painful for me too."

"So, going back to your new teacher, is he any good?"

"Matthias is the best teacher ever." Tamera wondered if Cassandra could sense the big smile on her face at that moment.

"The best?" Cassandra giggled. "You don't think that's a big statement to make after just one class?"

"Matthias is so smart," Tamera said. "And I'm not exaggerating."

"You keep calling him Matthias as if he's your good friend," Cassandra said with a smirk in her voice. "Should Dalton be worried?"

"You have a dirty mind," Tamera chortled. "I didn't say that I want to dump my boyfriend. I'm just trying to explain that he's an excellent teacher."

Later that evening, Tamera sat on her bed wondering what the initial *J* in Matthias's first name stood for. Joshua, Josiah, Joseph, John, Jeremy, Jonah, Jake, Jerry, Jason, Joel, Jaden. Her mind drew a blank, and she couldn't come up with more names that began with *J*. She put her phone on to charge and slid under her covers.

At the end of her second class, Tamera filed out of the room with the other students, just as she'd done on the first day. Matthias pulled up at almost the same spot. "Hop in," he beamed.

"Thanks," she smiled, this time getting in without hesitation.

"Want to tell me why you joined the class so late?"

"It's nothing really," she said. "It's boring stuff that you wouldn't be interested in."

"Try me," he said. "I don't think anything you tell me can possibly be boring."

"Well, to make a long story short, I wasn't sure I wanted to go back to school before the oil spill, but then I changed my mind. I want to get a good education so I can make a change in this community. Mathematics is the only CSEC subject I failed, so I'm working really hard to pass it. I also want to go back to school full-time next year to do CAPE."

"You're not just pretty, but you're smart too," he said.

His smile was wicked, Tamara thought. She grinned, pleased by the compliment.

"See you on Tuesday," he said, parking in front of her home. Again, he waited until she slipped through the front door before taking off.

The following day, a public holiday, Tamera phoned Azura. They hadn't spoken in over a month. "That's really great," Azura said when Tamera told her how much she was enjoying the evening mathematics class. "I'm so glad you decided to go back to school."

"Me too," Tamera said.

"It's a little bit scary how everything is quickly changing around us," Azura said. "The worst of all is you losing your mom, and I know you also miss Jan, but at least it's good to know that you have a plan in place for your life."

"How is university?"

"Well, I'm thoroughly enjoying it, and even though I didn't get the scholarship I was hoping for, I'm working my butt off, and maybe I'll get one to do my masters in the States."

"That's good to hear," Tamera said.

"We've got to keep in touch more often," Azura said.

Tamera put the phone away, and her thoughts flashed back to earlier, better days when her mother was alive and in good health. "Ma," she said softly to herself, "it's so hard to live without you right now."

The following day, Mary and her family returned home. And the day after that, Tamera promised her elder sister that she would babysit Emma.

"Thank you, Jesus." Cynthia stood on the porch with the phone to her ear as Tamera headed out of the house, clutching her math textbook.

"Looks like you got some good news," Earl said when Cynthia pocketed her phone.

"The police just confirmed that that body they found is not my daughter's." She smiled, pressing her hand against her chest. "The dental record wasn't a match."

Later that afternoon, Tamera shampooed her hair. Afterward, she carefully flat-ironed her shoulder-length hair in front of the full-length mirror behind the bathroom door. She was excited that Dalton was planning to visit La Cresta the following day. She hadn't seen him in over a month and she wanted to look her best when he arrived. She stood in front of the mirror combing her hair and imagining how they might spend their time together.

# 23.

DARK GLASSES CONCEALED Dalton's eyes, and his muscular arms popped out of a sleeveless, light blue T-shirt. "You look like a princess," he said and took off his sunglasses, resting them on the round table on Tamera family's porch.

"What's with the beard?" Tamera asked, standing next to him, grinning.

"I'm going to get rid of it this weekend." He stroked the tuft of hair on his chin. "How are you doing?"

"Good," she said.

"I'm really glad to see you."

"Me too," Tamera said as they gave each other a light hug.

"You know it's almost five weeks since you've been home, right?" she said.

"I know," he grimaced. "Life's not always how we want it, but we have to do the best with what we've got."

"What's wrong?" Tamera asked with concern.

"Nothing more than usual," he said. "You wanna go down to the beach?"

"We still can't swim there."

"I know. But we can enjoy the fresh air while we talk."

A mottled green cluster of trees stood in the background as the young couple strolled along the beach, holding hands. "I need to feel the water on my feet." Tamera broke loose, slipping off her sandals. Dalton remained on the shore, his eyes on her as she waded in the water. "Come on in," she beamed as she beckoned him to join her.

"No," he grinned.

All of a sudden, she bolted out of the water as if escaping a monster. "A catfish just washed ashore." She pointed to the dead animal. "Fewer fish are dying, but it hurts to see even one," she added as the fiery sand massaged the soles of her feet and the insides of her toes.

"It's going to take a long time for the pollution to subside," he said. She held her sandals with her right hand and his hand with her left. They strolled away from a tiny patch of oil shimmering on the sand. "Have you ever seen a dog eat raw fish?"

"No," she replied.

"Look." He pointed to a mangy dog clutching a dead moonshine between its teeth. "I have a lot of respect for men like Mr. Joshua and your Uncle Charlie who are trying so much to help the locals."

"But there's more to be done," she said. "The fishermen who own boats are getting some compensation from the government now, but their helpers aren't getting anything, and they have to feed their families too."

"It's going to take a very long time before things get back to normal," he said.

"I don't think it ever will, because the beach is a burial ground for so many fish and wildlife," she said. "It's never again going to be the innocent place where we spent our childhood."

"You're probably right about that."

They stood in one spot but continued to hold hands. "This disaster has changed you," he said as he looked her square in the face.

"You think?" she smiled.

"I can see it in your eyes," he said.

"The disaster has changed everybody in the community, not just me," Tamara replied matter-of-factly. She glanced around and said, "Look, no one's here except us."

He looked around too, then nodded. "Well, it's great that we have the beach all to ourselves, because I've got a surprise," he grinned. "But you've gotta catch me to know what it is."

He darted ahead and Tamera galloped after him, even though there was no way she could catch him unless he slowed down, which he eventually did.

"What is it?" she gasped, out of breath.

"I've got a confession to make."

"A confession?" she said with a piercing gaze.

"Well," he scowled. "I just didn't…"

"What is it?" she frowned. "You didn't come all the way here just to give me bad news, I hope."

"There are two things I've gotta do," he smiled. "The first is to give you this." He pulled a tiny square box from his pocket. "I've been working long hours to save up for it." He held up a gold chain with a delicate angel pendant. "Happy birthday," he said.

"But my birthday's not till next week."

"I can't be here then," he said. "So I don't have no choice but to give it to you right now."

She tilted her head, and he slipped it around her neck. "There," he said, clasping it in place.

"Thank you. It's beautiful," she said. She was surprised and happy, and she toyed with the pendant as they continued to walk along the beach. "I wish you could be here for my birthday, Dalton. We see so little of each other these days."

Dalton pursed his lips then turned around to face her. "I'm going to Toledo," he announced abruptly.

"Toledo?" Tamera was rooted to the spot. "What for?"

"My job's sending me there."

"For how long?"

"My boss offered me a promotion."

"You're moving there for good?" she asked, glaring at him.

"Look, Tammy," he said. "I know you're upset, but…"

"We hardly see each other now!" Tamera cried. "What's going to happen when you have to cross the sea to get here?"

"My boss made me an offer I couldn't refuse," he said. "One of the men in Toledo retired. Opportunities like this only come along once in a while. I got this promotion because my boss has confidence in me. You should be happy that my career is moving ahead so quickly." He paused for a moment. "Please don't look as if it's the end of the world. This is a good thing for me."

"You can do whatever you want," Tamera frowned, and tightly folded her arms across her chest.

"You've gotta look at the positives, not just the negatives," Dalton said. "Nothing happens in life without sacrifice. And I have to think about my future."

They walked back to his car in silence. Tamera was so upset by this news that she couldn't bring herself to say anything.

When they'd settled, Dalton tore open a bag of *channa* that he'd pulled out of the glove compartment. "Want some?" he said. The bag rustled as he opened it.

"Just a little," she said. He poured the beige legumes into the palm of her hand. "That's enough."

"That's less than a dozen you've got there." He grinned. "Isn't this one of your favourite snacks?"

"Yeah," she said softly, "but I'm not hungry right now."

He dumped a handful of the beans into his mouth, threw the bag on the dashboard, and switched on the ignition.

"This is it for now then," he said, parking in front of her home. "I promise you it's not going to be long before I come back home for another visit. Be happy for me."

She climbed out of the car without saying a word. She could barely bring herself to wave goodbye.

That evening, his text message read, *Arrived in San Pedro safely, but tired. Love, Dalton.*

The following morning, Earl knocked on Tamera's bedroom

door. "You're still asleep?" he said. "It's already ten o'clock, you know."

"Come in, Pa," she said. "I'm not sleeping."

"You're okay?" He walked in.

"I'm lying in bed, thinking."

"Anything you want to talk to me about?" He sat on the edge of the bed.

"Not really Pa." She sat up, propping herself with two pillows. She tried to smooth her rumpled hair. "Just thinking about Ma and how much I still miss her."

"I know it's tough to deal with the loss of your mother," he said. "When my mother died, I thought I'd never recover, but time was the best healer." His serious expression transformed into a bright smile. "I have some good news that going to cheer you up."

"Good news?"

"Yeah," he said. "I'm a grandfather for the second time 'round."

"Mary had the baby?" Tamera jumped to her feet. "That's so neat."

"He arrived at five this morning."

"Why didn't you wake me up?"

He chuckled. "When Renwick took your sister to the hospital at almost two this morning, you were out like a log, and frankly, there was nothing you could do to help."

"I guess not." She paused. "But what about Emma?"

"She in Mary's old room."

"I'm going to check on her," Tamera said, jumping out of bed and out her bedroom door.

Mary and her newborn son were discharged from the hospital the following morning.

"Come on. It's time to go home." Tamera held Emma's hand, leading her to the door.

"I'm going to meet you there in a little while," Earl said.

"Okay, Pa." Tamera headed down the staircase. Emma ran toward her mother, standing in the doorway. Mary hugged her firstborn and led her to the bedroom. "Come and see your little brother." Renwick scooped Emma off the floor, and carried her over to the sleeping infant. Emma stared at the baby blankly. As soon as her dad put her on the floor, she darted out of the room.

"He's so cute." Tamera eyes lit up. She gingerly stroked her nephew's arm. "He looks just like Emma when she was born," she said. The baby yawned and stretched without opening his eyes.

"Dad, you're here?" Mary said as Earl walked in the bedroom.

Earl grinned at Emma. "When you were born you had the same spiky hair and bushy eyebrows," he said. "My grandson brings back good memories of when both my girls were born."

"We're going to name him Howard after Renwick's dad," Mary said. "His middle name is in honour of you, Pa."

"Can I hold him?" Tamera stretched her arms to pick up the baby.

"Wait," Mary said. "Let me get him out of the crib." She gently lifted the child, her hand cupped protectively around his head. "Your hands are clean?"

"What do you mean if my hands are clean?" Tamera stuck out both arms.

"Sit on the couch, and I'm going to hand him over."

Tamera rolled her eyes. "I'm not going to drop him! Don't worry so much."

"Hold him carefully then." Mary placed the baby into Tamera's arms. Tamera walked to the living room, barely taking her eyes off her nephew's face. Earl, Renwick, and Mary followed.

"I wish Ma was here to meet you." Tamera's eyes remained on the baby's face.

Nobody noticed Emma hiding under the dining table. She crawled out from under the table and over to the corner of the room, pouting.

"Come and kiss your baby brother," Tamera said when she noticed her.

Emma stomped her feet. "No!" she screamed.

"Come here, sweetheart," Renwick cooed and picked her up.

"You behaved even worse than that when Tammy was born," Earl said, smiling at Mary. They all laughed.

# 24.

WHEN ALL GOVERNMENT SCHOOLS on the island nation closed for the two-week Christmas break, Jan remained in Port City, Charlie travelled to Toledo to vacation with friends, and Dalton couldn't come home for the holidays as he was too busy with the new job. It was one of the most uneventful Christmas seasons Tamera had ever spent in her life. and By the time school reopened in the New Year, she had already grown accustomed to getting a lift from Matthias at the end of each class. She'd linger in the deserted corridor waiting while he packed away his books and completed a few administrative tasks. They had started walking to the parking lot together rather then meeting further along the street.

"Let's go," he said and marched out of the classroom with a bulging multicoloured backpack slung over his left shoulder, and a big smile on his face. He trudged down the staircase ahead of her in his shiny black boots. As he pushed open the front door, a blue Toyota pulled out of the parking lot, leaving his car as the lone vehicle in the lot.

"You were very quiet today." Matthias dumped his backpack onto the rear seat. "You're okay?"

"Yeah." Tamera nodded.

"You didn't seem like yourself in class." He observed her grim face. She yielded to his prodding, admitting that she was sad because her boyfriend had moved to Toledo the previous day.

"You're very young," he said. "There's so much in life for

you to experience. Don't let that guy drag you down."

Tamera nodded and they drove the rest of the way home in companiable silence.

Tamera had become more and more relaxed in Matthias's company. After each class, they would converse in the deserted parking lot for about ten minutes before he took her home. Their conversations revolved entirely around her life and goals.

One day he uncharacteristically spoke about himself, telling her that he had gone to the United States to live with his mother when he was six years old. "I returned to Juniper almost a year ago," he said. "I didn't want to spend half the year bogged down in winter clothes when I could live in this beautiful island free from all those trappings. Believe me, the dead of winter is no fun."

"But Florida has nice weather most of the time," she said. "Why didn't you move there?"

"Not for a million dollars." He gestured with his hands. "Home is home. I'm doing fine right here, thank you very much."

"How are things?" Matthias said one Tuesday evening, adjusting his seatbelt. He clutched the steering wheel but didn't move the car.

"I'm okay," she frowned.

"Don't tell me that you're still thinking about that guy."

"No, I'm not," she replied adamantly.

"Good for you." He patted her arm. "I promise that no matter what you tell me, it'll stay right here."

That evening he shared another rare bit of information about himself. He told her that he had completed a bachelor's degree in mathematics and a master's degree in education at New York University. She thought his alma mater sounded like a wonderful university. It was the type of school she would love to attend in the future, but she didn't dare dream so big.

"You're the best math teacher ever," she exclaimed.

"Thanks," he smiled. "I wish your admiration regarding

my math teaching skills would translate into a full-time job, but I don't know if that'll ever happen." His face fell, and for a moment his thoughts seemed to go to a dark place. "Oh, well." He glanced at his oversized silver watch. "It's getting late." He swerved out of the parking lot and took her home.

A few weeks later, Tamera sat on her bed, staring incredulously at a text message she'd received minutes earlier from Dalton.

*Sorry, Tammy, but I've been thinking about what I'm going to say to you for a while now. I have to face the truth and come clean. I met someone, Alyssa, here in Toledo, and I now know that she is the right girl for me. I don't want you to find out from anyone else, so I'm telling you myself. Despite everything, we can still be friends.*

She re-read Dalton's text a second and then a third time. Anger boiled in her gut. As the soaring heat surged through her veins, she tugged the ring off her finger, and hurled it into the corner of the room. It bounced, making several dull sounds on the hardwood floor before rolling under the bed. She yanked the gold chain from her neck, and dumped the broken pieces at her feet. She stared at the text again, concentrating on the last five words.

*How can he expect us to be friends after this?*

Despite feeling awful, she had no intention of missing her evening class, though a lump formed in her throat. She took several deep breaths, and tried to pull herself together. "Dalton, you're not worth it," she said out loud, inhaling the fresh garden scent.

The lump in her throat got bigger, and her legs felt as if they would break. She gripped the bannister, slowly making her way down the staircase and forcing back tears. She cursed when she realized that she'd left her backpack behind. She rushed back up the stairs and into the house, picked up the backpack from the sofa where she'd left it, then threw it over her left shoulder, and stepped out the gate again.

"Watch out!" Edgar said in a husky voice as she accidentally bumped into him.

"Sorry." She felt the jab of something hard inside a crinkly brown paper bag he was holding. He brushed against her, and she stumbled, slipping off the curb. The brown bag hit the pavement.

"See what you did!" he roared, his foul stench seeping into her nostrils.

"Sorry," she said again as fragments of a broken bottle of rum spilled out of the soggy bag. Edgar glared at her and stumbled as he tried to grab her arm.

She hastily stepped back onto the pavement and with long, firm steps began to walk in the opposite direction from him, still feeling the effects of the sudden impact. For a moment she turned, staring at him, but quickly shifted focus to the brown bag on the side of the pavement and the jagged pieces of glass scattered around it. She knew she ought to turn back and pick up the sharp fragments in case someone should accidentally step on them, but she didn't because she was running late.

That evening, as usual, Matthias held the car door open for her. "How are things?" he said as she climbed in the car.

"Okay," she said with downcast eyes.

"You were very quiet in class again today." He held the steering wheel but didn't release the handbrake. "I can always tell when you're not yourself," he smiled and paused. "What is it?"

"I..." she said. "Never mind."

"Never mind what?" he said as she shed her first tears over the message she'd received from Dalton.

*Stupid me*, she thought, knotting her fingers together.

"I know that you're still thinking about that guy?"

"No, I'm not." She bowed, wiping her eyes with the back of her hand. "He's got another girlfriend now." She tried to stop herself from losing control, but the dam within her burst. The tears streamed down her cheeks.

"Here," he said gently as he handed her a tissue. She wiped

the slimy mucus running down her nostrils, and tried unsuc-cessfully to stem the flow of tears. "

"Look at me," he said, but she kept her head low.

"Let it out." He cupped her face. "Don't hold it inside," he said, guiding her head toward his shoulder. She kept it there, sobbing and heaving. He patted her back. She eventually got a hold of herself and sat upright.

"Feeling better now?"

She looked at him with gloomy eyes, nodding. She managed a smile, even though she wanted to die. Tamera needed to open up to someone she could trust about the text Dalton had sent her, and she did so now, confident that her story wouldn't circulate in the village. Afterward, he drove her home. "I promise that in time you'll be happy again," he said, pulling up to the curb in front of her gate. "See you next week," he said and waved.

"See you then," she said, and ran up the stairs and into her house.

That evening, Tamera lay in bed trying to get Dalton out of her thoughts, but she couldn't.

*Is his new girlfriend taller than me? Is she prettier that me? Has she emailed him revealing photos of herself? How long was he cheating before he dumped me?*

After tossing and turning in her bed for several minutes, Tamera sat up straight, propping herself up with a pillow. She picked up her phone from the night table and dialled Jan's number. "Sorry for calling you after eleven," Tamera's voice was shaking.

"What's going on in La Cresta?" Jan asked. "You don't sound like yourself."

"Dalton left me for some girl named Alyssa," Tamera blurted.

"What?" Jan asked. "When?"

"I got a text from him earlier today. You know what he said? That we could still be friends."

"Friends?" Jan huffed. "He's no friend."

"It's hurting a lot," Tamera sobbed. "How could he have met someone so soon?"

"He isn't worth crying over," Jan said. "He barely spent anytime with you anyhow."

"I really though we were going to be together forever," Tamera sobbed a little louder. "I feel like such a fool," she added.

"Don't be so hard on yourself 'cause he's not worth one drop of your tears. You're going to find someone better than him, someone who really loves you, and who wants to spend loads of time with you."

"Mary's gonna say I told you so. She's gonna make me feel worse than I feel now."

"Just tell her and everyone else that you broke off with him 'cause he lives so far away. I'm not gonna say anything about this to anybody, okay?"

"Okay, okay..." Tamera sighed. She ended the call and buried herself under the sheets, and then cried until she finally fell asleep.

At the end of the next class, Tamera and Matthias walked toward the parking lot in total silence. "Feeling better?" he said, holding the door.

"Yeah," she nodded, climbing into the car.

"You wanna know something?" He slipped into the driver's seat.

"What?" she said with a wry smile.

"I once had a girlfriend who I really loved, but she didn't really care about me." He frowned. "If she was anything like you, I'd probably still be living in the States today, but unfortunately she stabbed me in the back, causing me more grief that you could imagine."

"You left the States because of a girl?" she said. "I thought it was the cold weather you ran away from."

"You're a good listener." he said. "My old girlfriend betrayed me. But I'm glad she's out of my life, because then I wouldn't have met you." His eyes caught hers and for a moment Tamera was confused.

"I've wanted to do this for a very long time," he said softly and then gently kissed her. She remained motionless and silent. "I couldn't help myself," he said and sat upright. Tamera's thoughts were in a muddle. Her heart pounded and her hands felt clammy. She liked Matthias, but she was confused.

He leaned toward her again, holding her hand. He kissed her much slower than the first time. "I really care about you," he said, then paused. "I guess I'd better take you home before it's too late," he sighed.

He swerved out of the parking lot and minutes later pulled up in front of her home. "Sleep tight and think about me tonight. Don't let the bedbugs bite." He blew her a kiss. She smiled nervously, clumsily climbing out of the car. She looked back. He waved at her. He waited until she got to the top of the staircase before driving off.

That evening, Tamera was tempted to tell Cassandra and Jan about Matthias but she didn't. She felt a bit uneasy, but she couldn't wait for the next Tuesday when she would see him again.

Two days later, on Saturday, Tamera and Cassandra turned off Chester Street, walking toward Cassandra's home. "I'm so glad Dalton's out of my life," Tamera said as they approached his parents' house. The branches on the lone cashew tree in front of the dwelling waved forcefully in the robust wind.

"It's amazing." Cassandra snickered. "You seem so much happier than when you were still with him. You sure you haven't met someone else?"

"Maybe," Tamera giggled, waving at Cynthia, who was sitting on her porch. The girls strode past Cynthia's weed-infested garden.

"It's weird that hardly anybody talks 'bout LaToya anymore," Cassandra said. "Do you think she's still alive?"

"Well," Tamera said, "Miss Cynthia isn't giving up on her daughter, and I'm not giving up either."

"I often wonder if LaToya's a victim of human trafficking. We're hearing so much about that now."

"It's a scary thought," Tamera said as she headed up the terrazzo staircase at Cassandra's parents' home.

On Tuesday afternoon, after class had ended, Tamera and Matthias waited as usual for the parking lot to empty before walking to Matthias's car.

"Thank you," he said, sliding behind the wheel.

"For what?" she giggled. "I didn't do anything."

"Exactly that," he said. "I was a little bit worried that you might tell someone about us." He stroked the inside of her wrist. "Thanks so much for keeping our secret."

"I'll never tell anyone," she assured him.

"You're so sweet," he said and then cupped her face with his hands. "You're the best thing that's ever happened to me." His lips parted a little as he looked at her, remaining silent. He leaned to his side, and his lips touched the nape of her neck. Tamera shivered. Then she felt his breath as he kissed her squarely on the lips. "You're so different from all the other girls I've ever met," he said. "I want to invite you to my place in Port City, but I don't know if it will be possible for you to come without anyone finding out. You're going to accept my invitation?"

"I don't know." She twirled a handful of hair, smiling. "It's going to be really hard for me to go to Port City and not tell my dad."

"We can't let him know about us," he said. "Maybe you could tell him that you're going to the mall with some friends, and I could arrange to pick you up." He paused for a moment. "Gimme your number."

She did as he asked. "Let me sleep on it," Tamera said. "I need to think about this."

He added her number to his contacts. "I'll call you tomorrow after I come up with a solid plan."

"Okay," she said as he tangled his fingers with hers.

"I guess I'd better get you home right now," he said. They buckled their seatbelts and started on their way.

They were almost at Tamera's house when Matthias's face visibly tensed. A police cruiser was approaching them. "I wonder what they want?" he said, casting her an anxious look.

The police car pulled up alongside his vehicle. Two uniformed officers climbed out and the taller of the two strode to Matthias's window.

"How can I help you?" Matthias said. The shorter, stockier man walked in front of the car and stopped at the passenger's side window.

"Your license and registration please?" the law enforcement officer said.

"Here it is, sir," Matthias politely complied.

"You're Jonathan Thomas?" the officer said, inspecting the documents.

"Yes, sir."

"And the young lady?" The taller officer looked at her. "Your name?" he frowned.

"I'm Tamera Woods," she said.

"You're okay?"

"Yes," she nodded.

"How old are you?"

"Seventeen."

"You'd better get out of this car and find your way home," he said.

"I'll see you around," Matthias said as she nervously gathered her things.

She walked, almost ran, the rest of the way home, her heart beating in her ears. When she got to the sidewalk directly in front of her home, she finally looked back, watching as the officers handcuffed Matthias and led him toward their car.

Then she sat on the bottom step of the staircase, holding her chest. She took several deep breaths before deciding to go inside.

"You're back?" Earl was sitting on the recliner watching the evening news.

"Is there anything interesting on?" she asked politely.

"Not really." Earl kept his eyes on the television.

She walked to her room, sat on her bed and dialled Jan's number.

"How come you're calling me so late on a weekday?" Jan said.

"What I have to tell you can't wait." Tamera shared the details about Matthias's arrest, but she held back the particulars regarding their relationship.

"That's crazy," Jan said.

"He was looking really lost and scared when they put him in the car."

"Why do you think they arrested him?"

"I don't have a clue."

"The police wouldn't just arrest him unless he did something."

"I know that."

"Tammy," Jan said. "I've gotta finish studying for a biology test, but I 'll call you after school tomorrow."

Tamera charged her cell phone and lay in bed, reliving Matthias's arrest in her head. She shifted from her left to her right side, trying to get him out of her thoughts, but she couldn't. At one-thirty in the morning, she was still awake. She climbed out of bed and switched on her computer. She typed *J. Matthias Thomas* into the search engine, but none of the results that popped up related to him.

"Jonathan," she said, recalling the name that the police officer had called him.

*Jonathan Thomas.* She searched the name.

*Award-Winning Teacher Arrested For Sleeping With Underage Girl.* She was certain that the headline of the first story was about someone else with a similar name, but the title intrigued her, so she clicked on the link.

The first thing to catch her eyes was a photo of Matthias in a business suit accepting an award from a middle-aged woman at a New York School. The photo captured the Matthias she knew, not the man the article branded as a child molester. Her stomach twisted into tiny knots as she read the details about Jonathan Thomas's arrest and imprisonment for the statutory rape of two high school students. She printed the article out and placed it into her purse with trembling hands.

She went to sleep in tears.

She dragged herself out of bed at five the following morning. She stared into the bathroom mirror. Her puffy eyes made her look ten years older.

Mary knocked on her sister's bedroom door. "Tammy?" she said. "It's already eleven o'clock, you know."

"I'm not feeling so well," Tamera said softly.

"What wrong with you?" Mary stood at the foot of her sister's bed.

"The police arrested my teacher last night." Tamera sat up. "And you wouldn't believe what I found out about him online." She gave Mary the article she'd printed out.

"You've gotta be kidding me." Mary's eyes opened wide. "How come he got a teaching job in a government school?"

"I don't know." Tamera shrugged.

"Anyhow, what I came to ask you is if you could look after Emma for a few hours this afternoon, 'cause the baby's sick and I've gotta take him to the doctor."

"Not a problem," Tamera said. She got dressed, had a bite to eat, and then emailed the online article about Matthias to her closest friends before heading to her sister's place.

The following day, the *Juniper Express* detailed that Matthias had been arrested outside the La Cresta Secondary School on Thursday evening due to an alleged inappropriate relationship with an underage girl, a student he tutored at his home. And, as information regarding his previous conviction and deportation from the United States became widespread, the residents of La Cresta grew increasingly alarmed that the Ministry of Education had slipped up, hiring someone with his background. Villagers gossiped about his possible connection to LaToya's disappearance.

"Mr. Thomas has an air-tight alibi, and all speculation regarding his involvement in the La Cresta girl's disappearance is without merit," his lawyer tried without success to assure the public.

Tamera put on a brave face heading to her first class after Matthias's arrest. While walking to school days later, a car similar to his sped down the street. She flinched. *How could I have been so stupid?*

She still hadn't told anyone about what had happened between them. She felt sick to her stomach, so she recited her math formulas, trying to get him out of her thoughts.

That year, Samuel cancelled the annual wire-bending exhibition, and instead, the community came together to hold a vigil in honour of LaToya. Days later, Tamera and her friends attended the annual carnival festivities at the secondary school, but somehow it wasn't as fun as it had been the previous year.

As carnival became a distant memory, Tamera's father and his brother began to prepare for the annual family get-together at her home. Tamera's math exam was approaching too, and she was much more confident about her chances for success than before. Her math teacher, Kristen Griffiths, was still in her early twenties, but very knowledgeable. "I think you're good enough to get a distinction," Miss Griffiths had told Tamera after she aced the most recent test with a ninety percent score. Tamera still struggled with her emotions whenever Dalton slipped into her mind, but the wound caused by the breakup had healed considerably. She only thought of Matthias when someone else mentioned his name. Since then, she had vowed to be on her guard and never to be so naïve again.

# 25.

O N SATURDAY MORNING, Earl held up a shopping list. "You're coming?" he asked, looking across at his daughter.

"Yes, Pa." She was glad to get some fresh air. Recently, besides attending classes two evenings a week and visiting Cassandra on the odd occasion, she had lived an almost reclusive life. An outing to the supermarket was just what she needed. She and Earl and the rest of the family were getting ready for the annual get-together.

The supermarket door automatically slid apart and Earl wheeled the overflowing grocery cart toward his car. "I can hardly wait to get home and take a shower." Tamera put two bags in the back seat of her father's car, while Earl placed the rest into the trunk. The shopping had taken a bit longer than expected and it was another scorching day.

"Good," he said as he closed the trunk. He wiped the sweat pouring down his neck. Just before turning onto Chester Street, he swerved to accommodate a speeding ambulance.

He carefully rounded the corner, his eyes focused on a lime-green vehicle that had mounted the pavement in front of Joshua's house and a black car that had rear-ended it. A police cruiser blocked all traffic. Earl pulled to the side and stopped. He and Tamera joined the villagers who had already gathered a short distance from the collision.

"Edgar got hit, and it doesn't look too good," Joshua said as Earl walked toward him. "He lost a lot of blood, but hopefully he's going to pull through."

"He drinks too much!" one of the neighbours shouted.

"He's got strange ways, but he doesn't really bother nobody," another resident said.

The emergency medical technicians wheeled Edgar to the ambulance while the police officers interviewed witnesses. "This is what happens when people speed," one of the officers said to no one in particular.

Joshua told the police that he had heard a loud bang from inside his shop but didn't witness the impact.

"Where's his brother, Samuel?" Earl asked Joshua.

"He's not at home right now," Joshua said. "I tried to reach him by phone, but he's not answering, so I left him a message."

About three hours later, news reached the residents of La Cresta that Edgar had died. "It's a pity he had to go like that." Cynthia shook her head. She and Earl were drinking coffee on the porch. "He had his problems, but he really wasn't a horrible man," she added.

When Tamera joined them on the porch, her father told her about Edgar's death. Tamera's face drooped. She felt badly for him, especially because he'd suffered from mental health issues just like her mom. "He was a sad human being."

"He used to be a really good carpenter in his better days," Earl said. "He worked on this house more than twenty-five years ago, and he did a good job."

"I wish I could have done more for my brother, but trying to reason with him was a battle I could never win," Samuel said. He and Earl were standing outside, facing the high wall Edgar had built after they'd fallen out.

"You're going to take care of the funeral arrangements?" Earl said.

"Not at all," Samuel said. "I'm waiting for his daughter, Kay, to come from Toledo to organize things." He sipped on a bottle of water. "Edgar accused me of stealing from him, and I don't want Kay to have any chance to say the same thing."

Tamera felt sorry that her aunt, Leila, was unable to attend the family function, but she was anxious to see Jan and Azura. Her two favourite cousins were among the first guests to arrive. The three of them limed under a big white tent. They were happy to see each other and be together.

"I read in the papers yesterday that Matthias got bail," Azura said.

"I hope they find him guilty and that he goes to jail for a long time," Jan said. "I bet you he's the person who hurt LaToya."

"I don't think it's him," Azura said. "What do you think, Tammy?"

"I don't know," she said and then burst into tears.

"What's the matter?" Azura handed her a tissue.

Tamera bit her lip. "I'm thinking about my mom," she lied, wiping her eyes. "This is the first family get-together since she died."

"I'm so sorry," Azura said. "I wish there was something I could do."

"Don't worry." Tamera forced a smile. "I'm going to be all right."

Even though she missed her mother, it was her time with Matthias that was weighing her down. She needed to share her innermost thoughts with someone, but it wasn't the right place or time.

She and her two cousins had an excellent view of the massive structure that was nearing completion on the land her father had sold to the returning nationals, the Edwards. "As you can see, our new neighbours are going to move in very soon," Tamera said.

"You still keep in touch with their son, Kyle?" Jan asked.

"Yeah," Azura said and sipped on lemonade. "We exchange emails once in a while."

A white Volkswagen parked in front of Edgar's house, and a tiny woman with short-cropped hair climbed out of the car ahead of a tall man. Two bright red suitcases bounced on the ground as a lofty gentleman wheeled them from the car toward the gate.

"Isn't that Edgar's daughter, Kay?" Jan said.

"It looks a lot like her." Tamera sat up straight. "But it's so sad that she waited till now to show her face."

"We don't know all the facts," Azura said. "So it's not fair for us to lay blame."

It was a couple of hours later, when they noticed Samuel running out of his house and down his staircase. "What's up with him?" Tamera kept her eyes on him as he darted toward his deceased brother's house.

Minutes later, a wailing police cruiser parked on Chester Street in front of Edgar's house. Two cops jumped out of the vehicle and burst through the gate. An ambulance raced down Chester Street next and pulled up directly behind the police cruiser.

"Let's go see what's going on over there," Tamera said and jumped off her chair. Her cousins followed. They joined a growing crowd on the pavement opposite Edgar's dwelling. Two emergency medical technicians emerged from the gate with someone lying on a stretcher, covered with a blanket.

"What's all this commotion about?" Earl asked as he walked toward the throngs of people on the pavement, many of whom had filed out of the family get-together. He stood next to Joshua.

"Stay over there!" A police officer gestured for the spectators to keep their distance from the ambulance.

"Is that LaToya?" a big voice yelled from the middle of the crowd.

"It sure looks like her," Jan cried out.

"Wow!" Tamera's eyes opened wide. Her jaw dropped.

Samuel strode out of the gate. "What going on, man?" Joshua and Earl waved at him. The three men met in the middle of the street.

"The girl," Samuel grimaced and pointed. "Kay's husband found her chained up like a hog in one of Edgar's bedrooms. Thank God he's a police officer and easily took charge of things. She's in pretty bad shape. It baffles me how my brother could have been so cruel to another human being. I don't understand."

"Christ, man!" Joshua scowled. "You're telling me she been right there all this time, and nobody knew what was going on?"

"This is crazy," Earl grumbled, shaking his head.

"I know it's bad," Samuel said. "But I haven't been at my brother's place in more than a year, and I didn't have a clue what was going on."

Three weeks after LaToya was discharged from Port City General Hospital, she was finally ready to meet well-wishers. Tamera and Earl were among her first visitors. "I'm so sorry," Tamera said, embracing her former classmate, grateful that she'd been found and was on the mend.

"I'm alive." LaToya smiled weakly. "Don't look at me as if you're at a wake." She was considerably thinner and spoke much softer and slower than before she'd been taken. Her mother joined Earl on the porch, and Tamera followed her to the living room.

"How are you doing?" Tamera said as they sat down next to each other.

"I don't want to talk 'bout myself right now." LaToya pulled her feet up on the sofa, exposing an unsightly scar wrapped around her right ankle. Tamera didn't know what to say after that.

# 26.

CYNTHIA PLANTED CACTI and succulents throughout the perimeter of her garden. She uprooted the weeds, shaped the shrubs, and pruned the trees. At about ten on a Saturday morning, Charlie parked his brand-new Audi at her gate. He honked twice. LaToya leapt out of the living room. Cynthia followed her daughter onto the porch. They hugged. LaToya trotted happily toward the car, turned around and waved. Jan and Tamera shifted in the back seat to make room for her. Cynthia waved happily at the occupants of the car.

"Hi, everyone." LaToya's lively voice was back, and her skin glowed like it used to before she'd vanished.

"You're okay?" Azura said from the front passenger seat.

"Everything's neat." La Toya buckled her seat belt.

Charlie turned the car around, and Tamera scowled, observing a woman with a beautifully dolled-up face in the front passenger seat of Dalton's car as he backed out of his parents' yard. She didn't say anything. The others remained silent too. Charlie and his passengers were on their way to the north of the island. He drove along meandering hills, while upbeat music poured out of the car's stereo, keeping them awake.

"We're here," Charlie announced as a rich array of foliage surrounded them.

"Wow! It's real nice up here," Tamera said, as a swarm of monarch butterflies fluttered around them. Days earlier, she'd registered for CAPE classes and was looking forward to heading

196

back to school full-time in September, having achieved grade one in her CSEC mathematics examination.

Charlie, Jan, and Azura walked ahead of Tamera and LaToya at the three-hundred-acre nature resort, one of the top bird-watching spots in the Caribbean, with more than one hundred and fifty species of birds. Charlie pointed to a tiny bird with a straight black bill, golden-green upperparts, white underparts and a bronze tail, tipped purple-blue. "That's a white-chested emerald hummingbird," he said.

While they admired the myriad birds hovering around bird-feeders, Azura said she wished she owned a long-lensed camera similar to the one a tourist next to her was using.

By that time, it was well known in the community that Edgar had snatched LaToya from behind his house moments after she wandered there alone. He'd dragged her inside through a back door. Hours later, she awoke groggily with duct tape over her mouth, her hands and feet shackled with a rusty chain to a pole in his bedroom.

"Come on," Tamera gestured, waiting for LaToya to catch up to her. They had in recent times developed a close bond. Tamera was the only person, besides LaToya's counsellor, with detailed knowledge of the abuse she'd suffered during her captivity at Edgar's house. Tamera knew specifics that LaToya had not even shared with her mom.

Tamera bit her lip, recalling the support she'd received from LaToya after sharing her own difficulties during the past year. She had confided in her about the loss of her mother, the breakup with Dalton, and the betrayal she felt after learning who Matthias really was. She grimaced, recalling the horrors Edgar had inflicted on her friend, but she managed a smile, too, reminding herself that LaToya had the strong-willed character to make a full recovery.

When LaToya caught up to Tamera, a mango hummingbird whizzed by her left ear, but she didn't notice the tiny creature, its rainbow-like colours bouncing off its feathers as it fluttered through the air. The little bird flew upside down and shifted sideways as it glided toward a cluster of leafy green plants in search of flower nectar. LaToya threw a thick, long braid off her face and exclaimed, "They're beautiful!"

Tamera nodded. She too was admiring the stunning winged creatures fluttering around birdfeeders and the lush rainforest in the distance, imagining she was enjoying a little piece of heaven. She suddenly felt a lump in her throat, and her eyes misted over, and she knew she would do everything she could to protect this place, always.

# Acknowledgements

First, I'd like to thank God for planting the passion in me to pursue my dreams. I could never have completed this book without my faith in you.

Thank you to my friends and relatives for your kind words of encouragement. I am especially grateful to my childhood friend, Debra Howell, and my sister, Caroline Guevara, who have gone overboard to support me as a writer.

To my mother and father, thank you so much for your love. I miss you and wish you were able to share this wonderful experience with me.

I wish to acknowledge the fishermen at Las Cuevas beach, Trinidad who eagerly answered all of my questions. The information you shared was vital to completing this book.

I am indebted to Inanna Publications. Thank you Val Fullard for the cover design and thank you also to Renée Knapp, Publicist and Marketing Manager, and especially, to Luciana Ricciutelli, Editor-in-Chief.

*Photo: John Burridge*

Glynis Guevara was born in Barataria, Trinidad and Tobago. She holds a Bachelor of Law (Hons.) degree from the University of London, England, and is a graduate of Humber School for Writers creative writing program. Glynis was admitted to the bar of England and Wales, and Trinidad and Tobago. She was shortlisted for the Small Axe Literary short fiction prize in 2012 and the inaugural Burt Award for Caribbean literature in 2014. She currently works as an adult literacy instructor in Toronto. Her debut young adult novel, *Under the Zaboca Tree,* was published by Inanna Publications in 2017. Visit her website at: www.glynisguevara.com.